There's the blip!
    It's crazy!
        Nothing can go that fast!

Jed Cochrane was a television producer with strictly Earthy tastes. When he was sent to Lunar City to publicize the apparently worthless discovery of his boss' inventive son-in-law, Jed was furious. As his anger grew to universal proportions, so did his involvement in young Dabney's discovery. If the fledgling scientist were right, man could travel faster than the speed of light—but the theory still had to be proven. And, of course, Jed was chosen to test the space-shaking equation!

Before he could say "Einstein," Jed found himself trapped inside a spacecraft with his kooky secretary, Babs Deane, and a reluctant psychiatrist, Bill Holden, being hurled far beyond the confines of the Solar System towards a planet inhabited by bizarre creatures—a volcanic world strangely similar to Earth itself!

SIGNET Science Fiction Books
You Will Enjoy

Operation:
Outer Space

By Murray Leinster

A SIGNET BOOK
Published by The New American Library

Published as a SIGNET BOOK by arrangement with
Fantasy Press

THIRD PRINTING

SIGNET TRADEMARK REG. U.S. PAT. OFF. AND FOREIGN COUNTRIES
REGISTERED TRADEMARK—MARCA REGISTRADA
HECHO EN CHICAGO, U.S.A.

SIGNET BOOKS are published by
The New American Library, Inc.,
1301 Avenue of the Americas, New York, New York 10019

FIRST PRINTING, APRIL, 1957

PRINTED IN THE UNITED STATES OF AMERICA

CHAPTER ONE

JED COCHRANE TRIED TO BE CYNICAL AS THE HELICAB hummed softly through the night over the city. The cab flew at two thousand feet, where lighted buildings seemed to soar toward it from the canyons which were streets. There were lights and people everywhere, and Cochrane sardonically reminded himself that he was no better than anybody else, only he'd been trying to keep from realizing it. He looked down at the trees and shrubbery on the roof-tops, and at a dance that was going on atop one of the tallest buildings. All roofs were recreation-spaces nowadays. They were the only spaces available. When you looked down at a city like this, you had cynical thoughts. Fourteen million people in this city. Ten million in that. Eight in another and ten in another still, and twelve million in yet another ... Big cities. Swarming millions of people, all desperately anxious—so Cochrane realized bitterly—all desperately anxious about their jobs and keeping them.

"Even as me and I," said Cochrane harshly to himself. "Sure! I'm shaking in my shoes right along with the rest of them!"

But it hurt to realize that he'd been kidding himself. He'd thought he was important. Important, at least, to the advertising firm of Kursten, Kasten, Hopkins and Fallowe. But right now he was on the way—like a common legman—to take the moon-rocket to Lunar City, and he'd been informed of it just thirty minutes ago. Then he'd been told casually to get to the rocket-port right away. His secretary and two technical men and a writer were taking the same rocket. He'd get his instructions from Dr. William Holden on the way.

A part of his mind said indignantly, "*Wait till I get Hopkins on the phone! It was a mixup! He wouldn't send me off anywhere with the Dikkipatti Hour depending on me! He's not that crazy!*" But he was on his way

5

to the space-port, regardless. He'd raged when the message reached him. He'd insisted that he had to talk to Hopkins in person before he obeyed any such instructions. But he was on his way to the space-port. He was riding in a helicab, and he was making adjustments in his own mind to the humiliation he unconsciously foresaw. There were really three levels of thought in his mind. One had adopted a defensive cynicism, and one desperately insisted that he couldn't be as unimportant as his instructions implied, and the third watched the other two as the helicab flew with cushioned booming noises over the dark canyons of the city and the innumerable lonely lights of the rooftops.

There was a thin roaring sound, high aloft. Cochrane jerked his head back. The stars filled all the firmament, but he knew what to look for. He stared upward.

One of the stars grew brighter. He didn't know when he first picked it out, but he knew when he'd found it. He fixed his eyes on it. It was a very white star, and for a space of minutes it seemed in no wise different from its fellows. But it grew brighter. Presently it was very bright. It was brighter than Sirius. In seconds more it was brighter than Venus. It increased more and more rapidly in its brilliance. It became the brightest object in all the heavens except the crescent moon, and the cold intensity of its light was greater than any part of that. Then Cochrane could see that this star was not quite round. He could detect the quarter-mile-long flame of the rocket-blast.

It came down with a rush. He saw the vertical, stabbing pencil of light plunge earthward. It slowed remarkably as it plunged, with all the flying aircraft above the city harshly lighted by its glare. The space-port itself showed clearly. Cochrane saw the buildings, and the other moon-rockets waiting to take off in half an hour or less.

The white flame hit the ground and splashed. It spread out in a wide flat disk of intolerable brightness. The sleek hull of the ship which still rode the flame down glinted vividly as it settled into the inferno of its own making.

Then the light went out. The glare cut off abruptly. There was only a dim redness where the space-port tarmac had been made incandescent for a little while. That glow faded—and Cochrane became aware of the enormous stillness. He had not really noticed the rocket's deafening roar until it ended.

The helicab flew onward almost silently, with only the throbbing pulses of its overhead vanes making any sound at all.

"I kidded myself about those rockets, too," said Cochrane bitterly to himself. *"I thought getting to the moon meant starting to the stars. New worlds to live on. I had a lot more fun before I found out the facts of life!"*

But he knew that this cynicism and this bitterness came out of the hurt to the vanity that still insisted everything was a mistake. He'd received orders which disillusioned him about his importance to the firm and to the business to which he'd given years of his life. It hurt to find out that he was just another man, just another expendable. Most people fought against making the discovery, and some succeeded in avoiding it. But Cochrane saw his own self-deceptions with a savage clarity even as he tried to keep them. He did not admire himself at all.

The helicab began to slant down toward the space-port buildings. The sky was full of stars. The earth—of course —was covered with buildings. Except for the space-port there was no unoccupied ground for thirty miles in any direction. The cab was down to a thousand feet. To five hundred. Cochrane saw the just-arrived rocket with tender-vehicles running busily to and fro and hovering around it. He saw the rocket he should take, standing upright on the faintly lighted field.

The cab touched ground. Cochrane stood up and paid the fare. He got out and the cab rose four or five feet and flitted over to the waiting-line.

He went into the space-port building. He felt himself growing more bitter still. Then he found Bill Holden— Doctor William Holden—standing dejectedly against a wall.

"I believe you've got some orders for me, Bill," said Cochrane sardonically. "And just what psychiatric help can I give you?"

Holden said tiredly:

"I don't like this any better than you do, Jed. I'm scared to death of space-travel. But go get your ticket and I'll tell you about it on the way up. It's a special production job. I'm roped in on it too."

"Happy holiday!" said Cochrane, because Holden looked about as miserable as a man could look.

He went to the ticket desk. He gave his name. On request, he produced identification. Then he said sourly:

"While you're working on this I'll make a phone-call."

He went to a pay visiphone. And again there were different levels of awareness in his mind—one consciously and defensively cynical, and one frightened at the revelation of his unimportance, and the third finding the others an unedifying spectacle.

He put the call through with an over-elaborate confidence which he angrily recognized as an attempt to deceive himself. He got the office. He said calmly:

"This is Jed Cochrane. I asked for a visiphone contact with Mr. Hopkins."

He had a secretary on the phone-screen. She looked at memos and said pleasantly:

"Oh, yes. Mr. Hopkins is at dinner. He said he couldn't be disturbed, but for you to go on to the moon according to your instructions, Mr. Cochrane."

Cochrane hung up and raged, with one part of his mind. Another part—and he despised it—began to argue that after all, he had better wait before thinking there was any intent to humiliate him. After all, his orders must have been issued with due consideration. The third part disliked the other two parts intensely—one for raging without daring to speak, and one for trying to find alibis for not even raging. He went back to the ticket-desk. The clerk said heartily:

"Here you are! The rest of your party's already on board, Mr. Cochrane. You'd better hurry! Takeoff's in five minutes."

Holden joined him. They went through the gate and got into the tender-vehicle that would rush them out to the rocket. Holden said heavily:

"I was waiting for you and hoping you wouldn't come. I'm not a good traveller, Jed."

The small vehicle rushed. To a city man, the dark expanse of the space-port was astounding. Then a spidery metal framework swallowed the tender-truck, and them. The vehicle stopped. An elevator accepted them and lifted an indefinite distance through the night, toward the stars. A sort of gangplank with a canvas siderail reached out across emptiness. Cochrane crossed it, and found himself at the bottom of a spiral ramp inside the rocket's passenger-compartment. A stewardess looked at the tickets. She led the way up, and stopped.

"This is your seat, Mr. Cochrane," she said professionally. "I'll strap you in this first time. You'll do it later."

Cochrane lay down in a contour-chair with an eight-inch mattress of foam rubber. The stewardess adjusted straps. He thought bitter, ironic thoughts. A voice said:

"Mr. Cochrane!"

He turned his head. There was Babs Deane, his secretary, with her eyes very bright. She regarded him from a contour-chair exactly opposite his. She said happily:

"Mr. West and Mr. Jamison are the science men, Mr. Cochrane. I got Mr. Bell as the writer."

"A great triumph!" Cochrane told her. "Did you get any idea what all this is about? Why we're going up?"

"No," admitted Babs cheerfully. "I haven't the least idea. But I'm going to the moon! It's the most wonderful thing that ever happened to me!"

Cochrane shrugged his shoulders. Shrugging was not comfortable in the straps that held him. Babs was a good secretary. She was the only one Cochrane had ever had who did not try to make use of her position as secretary to the producer of the Dikkipatti Hour on television. Other secretaries had used their nearness to him to wangle acting or dancing or singing assignments on other and lesser shows. As a rule they lasted just four public appearances before they were back at desks, spoiled for further secretarial use by their taste of fame. But Babs hadn't tried that. Yet she'd jumped at a chance for a trip to the moon.

A panel up toward the nose of the rocket—the upper end of this passenger compartment—glowed suddenly. Flaming red letters said, *"Takeoff, ninety seconds."*

Cochrane found an ironic flavor in the thought that splendid daring and incredible technology had made his coming journey possible. Heroes had ventured magnificently into the emptiness beyond Earth's atmosphere. Uncountable millions of dollars had been spent. Enormous intelligence and infinite pains had been devoted to making possible a journey of two hundred thirty-six thousand miles through sheer nothingness. This was the most splendid achievement of human science—the reaching of a satellite of Earth and the building of a human city there.

And for what? Undoubtedly so that one Jed Cochrane could be ordered by telephone, by somebody's secretary, to go and get on a passenger-rocket and get to the moon. Go—having failed to make a protest because his boss

9

wouldn't interrupt dinner to listen—so he could keep his job by obeying. For this splendid purpose, scientists had labored and dedicated men had risked their lives.

Of course, Cochrane reminded himself with conscious justice, of course there was the very great value of moon-mail cachets to devotees of philately. There was the value of the tourist facilities to anybody who could spend that much money for something to brag about afterward. There were the solar-heat mines—running at a slight loss —and various other fine achievements. There was even a night-club in Lunar City where one highball cost the equivalent of—say—a week's pay for a secretary like Babs. And—

The panel changed its red glowing sign. It said: *"Take-off forty-five seconds."*

Somewhere down below a door closed with a cushioned soft definiteness. The inside of the rocket suddenly seemed extraordinarily still. The silence was oppressive. It was dead. Then there came the whirring of very many electric fans, stirring up the air.

The stewardess' voice came matter-of-factly from below him in the upended cylinder which was the passenger-space.

"We take off in forty-five seconds. You will find yourself feeling very heavy. There is no cause to be alarmed. If you observe that breathing is oppressive, the oxygen content of the air in this ship is well above earth-level, and you will not need to breathe so deeply. Simply relax in your chair. Everything has been thought of. Everything has been tested repeatedly. You need not disturb yourself at all. Simply relax."

Silence. Two heart-beats. Three.

There was a roar. It was a deep, booming, numbing roar that came from somewhere outside the rocket's hull. Simultaneously, something thrust Cochrane deep into the foam-cushions of his contour-chair. He felt the cushion piling up on all sides of his body so that it literally surrounded him. It resisted the tendency of his arms and legs and abdomen to flatten out and flow sidewise, to spread him in a thin layer over the chair in which he rested.

He felt his cheeks dragged back. He was unduly conscious of the weight of objects in his pockets. His stomach pressed hard against his backbone. His sensations were

10

those of someone being struck a hard, prolonged blow all over his body.

It was so startling a sensation, though he'd read about it, that he simply stayed still and blankly submitted to it. Presently he felt himself gasp. Presently, again, he noticed that one of his feet was going to sleep. He tried to move it and succeeded only in stirring it feebly. The roaring went on and on and on . . .

The red letters in the panel said: *"First stage ends in five seconds."*

By the time he'd read it, the rocket hiccoughed and stopped. Then he felt a surge of panic. He was falling! He had no weight! It was the sensation of a suddenly dropping elevator a hundred times multiplied. He bounced out of the depression in the foam-cushion. He was prevented from floating away only by the straps that held him.

There was a sputter and a series of jerks. Then he had weight again as roarings began once more. This was not the ghastly continued impact of the take-off, but still it was weight—considerably greater weight than the normal weight of Earth. Cochrane wiggled the foot that had gone to sleep. Pins and needles lessened their annoyance as sensation returned to it. He was able to move his arms and hands. They felt abnormally heavy, and he experienced an extreme and intolerable weariness. He wanted to go to sleep.

This was the second-stage rocket-phase. The moon-rocket had blasted off at six gravities acceleration until clear of atmosphere and a little more. Acceleration-chairs of remarkably effective design, plus the pre-saturation of one's blood with oxygen, made so high an acceleration safe and not unendurable for the necessary length of time it lasted. Now, at three gravities, one did not feel on the receiving end of a violent thrust, but one did feel utterly worn out and spent. Most people stayed awake through the six-gravity stage and went heavily to sleep under three gravities.

Cochrane fought the sensation of fatigue. He had not liked himself for accepting the orders that had brought him here. They had been issued in bland confidence that he had no personal affairs which could not be abandoned to obey cryptic orders from the secretary of a boss he had actually never seen. He felt a sort of self-contempt which it would have been restful to forget in three-grav-

11

ity sleep. But he grimaced and held himself awake to contemplate the unpretty spectacle of himself and his actions.

The red light said: *"Second stage ends ten seconds."*

And in ten seconds the rockets hiccoughed once more and were silent, and there was that sickening feeling of free fall, but he grimly made himself think of it as soaring upward instead of dropping—which was the fact, too—and waited until the third-stage rockets boomed suddenly and went on and on and on.

This was nearly normal acceleration; the effect of this acceleration was the feel of nearly normal weight. He felt about as one would feel in Earth in a contour-chair tilted back so that one faced the ceiling. He knew approximately where the ship would be by this time, and it ought to have been a thrill. Cochrane was hundreds of miles above Earth and headed eastward out and up. If a port were open at this height, his glance should span continents.

No . . . The ship had taken off at night. It would still be in Earth's shadow. There would be nothing at all to be seen below, unless one or two small patches of misty light which would be Earth's too-many great cities. But overhead there would be stars by myriads and myriads, of every possible color and degree of brightness. They would crowd each other for room in which to shine. The rocket-ship was spiralling out and out and up and up, to keep its rendezvous with the space platform.

The platform, of course, was that artificial satellite of Earth which was four thousand miles out and went around the planet in a little over four hours, travelling from west to east. It had been made because to break the bonds of Earth's gravity was terribly costly in fuel—when a ship had to accelerate slowly to avoid harm to human cargo. The space platform was a filling station in emptiness, at which the moon-rocket would refuel for its next and longer and much less difficult journey of two hundred thirty-odd thousand miles.

The stewardess came up the ramp, moving briskly. She stopped and glanced at each passenger in each chair in turn. When Cochrane turned his open eyes upon her, she said soothingly:

"There's no need to be disturbed. Everything is going perfectly."

"I'm not disturbed," said Cochrane. "I'm not even nervous. I'm perfectly all right."

"But you should be drowsy!" she observed, concerned. "Most people are. If you nap you'll feel better for it."

She felt his pulse in a business-like manner. It was normal.

"Take my nap for me," said Cochrane, "or put it back in stock. I don't want it. I'm perfectly all right."

She considered him carefully. She was remarkably pretty. But her manner was strictly detached. She said:

"There's a button. You can reach it if you need anything. You may call me by pushing it."

He shrugged. He lay still as she went on to inspect the other passengers. There was nothing to do and nothing to see. Travellers were treated pretty much like parcels, these days. Travel, like television entertainment and most of the other facilities of human life, was designed for the seventy-to-ninety-per-cent of the human race whose likes and dislikes and predilections could be learned exactly by surveys. Anybody who didn't like what everybody liked, or didn't react like everybody reacted, was subject to annoyances. Cochrane resigned himself to them.

The red light-letters changed again, considerably later. This time they said: *"Free flight, thirty seconds."*

They did not say "free fall," which was the technical term for a rocket coasting upward or downward in space. But Cochrane braced himself, and his stomach-muscles were tense when the rockets stopped again and stayed off. The sensation of continuous fall began. An electronic speaker beside his chair began to speak. There were other such mechanisms beside each other passenger-chair, and the interior of the rocket filled with a soft murmur which was sardonically like choral recitation.

"The sensation of weightlessness you now experience," said the voice soothingly, *"is natural at this stage of your flight. The ship has attained its maximum intended speed and is still rising to meet the space platform. You may consider that we have left atmosphere and its limitations behind. Now we have spread sails of inertia and glide on a wind of pure momentum toward our destination. The feeling of weightlessness is perfectly normal. You will be greatly interested in the space platform. We will reach it in something over two hours of free flight. It is an artificial satellite, with an air-lock our ship will enter for refueling. You will be able to leave the ship and move about*

13

inside the Platform, to lunch if you choose, to buy souve-
nirs and mail them back and to view Earth from a height
of four thousand miles through quartz-glass windows.
Then, as now, you will feel no sensation of weight. You
will be taken on a tour of the space platform if you wish.
There are rest-rooms—."

Cochrane grimly endured the rest of the taped lecture.
He thought sourly to himself: *"I'm a captive audience*
without even an interest in the production tricks."

Presently he saw Bill Holden's head. The psychiatrist
had squirmed inside the straps that held him, and now
was staring about within the rocket. His complexion was
greenish.

"I understand you're to brief me," Cochrane told him,
"on the way up. Do you want to tell me now what all
this is about? I'd like a nice dramatic narrative, with
gestures."

Holden said sickly:

"Go to hell, won't you?"

His head disappeared. Space-nausea was, of course, as
definite an ailment as seasickness. It came from no weight.
But Cochrane seemed to be immune. He turned his mind
to the possible purposes of his journey. He knew nothing
at all. His own personal share in the activities of Kursten,
Kasten, Hopkins and Fallowe—the biggest advertising
agency in the world—was the production of the Dikkipatti Hour, top-talent television show, regularly every
Wednesday night between eight-thirty and nine-thirty
o'clock central U. S. time. It was a good show. It was
among the ten most popular shows on three continents.
It was not reasonable that he be ordered to drop it and
take orders from a psychiatrist, even one he'd known
unprofessionally for years. But there was not much, these
days, that really made sense.

In a world where cities with populations of less than
five millions were considered small towns, values were
peculiar. One of the deplorable results of living in a
world over-supplied with inhabitants was that there were
too many people and not enough jobs. When one had
a good job, and somebody higher up than oneself gave
an order, it was obeyed. There was always somebody
else or several somebodies waiting for every job there
was—hoping for it, maybe praying for it. And if a good
job was lost, one had to start all over.

This task might be anything. It was not, however, connected in any way with the weekly production of the Dik-kipatti Hour. And if that production were scamped this week because Cochrane was away, he would be the one to take the loss in reputation. The fact that he was on the moon wouldn't count. It would be assumed that he was slipping. And a slip was not good. It was definitely not good!

"I could do a documentary right now," Cochrane told himself angrily, *"titled 'Man-afraid-of-his-job.' I could make a very authentic production. I've got the material!"*

He felt weight for a moment. It was accompanied by booming noises. The sounds were not in the air outside, because there was no air. They were reverberations of the rocket-motors themselves, transmitted to the fabric of the ship. The ship's steering-rockets were correcting the course of the vessel and—yes, there was another surge of power—nudging it to a more correct line of flight to meet the space platform coming up from behind. The platform went around the world six times a day, four thousand miles out. During three of its revolutions anybody on the ground, anywhere, could spot it in daylight as an infinitesimal star, bright enough to be seen against the sky's blueness, rising in the west and floating eastward to set at the place of sunrise.

There was again weightlessness. A rocket-ship doesn't burn its rocket-engines all the time. It runs them to get started, and it runs them to stop, but it does not run them to travel. This ship was floating above the Earth, which might be a vast sunlit ball filling half the universe below the rocket, or might be a blackness as of the Pit. Cochrane had lost track of time, but not of the shattering effect of being snatched from the job he knew and thought important, to travel incredibly to do something he had no idea of. He felt, in his mind, like somebody who climbs stairs in the dark and tries to take a step that isn't there. It was a shock to find that his work wasn't important even in the eyes of Kursten, Kasten, Hopkins and Fallowe. That he didn't count. That nothing counted . . .

There was another dull booming outside and another touch of weight. Then the rocket floated on endlessly.

A long time later, something touched the ship's outer hull. It was a definite, positive clanking sound. And then there was the gentlest and vaguest of tuggings, and Cochrane could feel the ship being maneuvered. He knew it

15

had made contact with the space platform and was being drawn inside its lock.

There was still no weight. The stewardess began to unstrap the passengers one by one, supplying each with magnetic-soled slippers. Cochrane heard her giving instructions in their use. He knew the air-lock was being filled with air from the huge, globular platform. In time the door at the back—bottom—base of the passenger-compartment opened. Somebody said flatly:

"Space platform! The ship will be in this air-lock for some three hours plus for refueling. Warning will be given before departure. Passengers have the freedom of the platform and will be given every possible privilege."

The magnetic-soled slippers did hold one's feet to the spiral ramp, but one had to hold on to a hand-rail to make progress. On the way down to the exit door, Cochrane encountered Babs. She said breathlessly:

"I can't believe I'm really here!"

"I can believe it," said Cochrane, "without even liking it particularly. Babs, who told you to come on this trip? Where'd all the orders come from?"

"Mr. Hopkins' secretary," said Babs happily. "She didn't tell me to come. I managed that! She said for me to name two science men and two writers who could work with you. I told her one writer was more than enough for any production job, but you'd need me. I assumed it was a production job. So she changed the orders and here I am!"

"Fine!" said Cochrane. His sense of the ironic deepened. He'd thought he was an executive and reasonably important. But somebody higher up than he was had disposed of him with absent-minded finality, and that man's secretary and his own had determined all the details, and he didn't count at all. He was a pawn in the hands of firm-partners and assorted secretaries. "Let me know what my job's to be and how to do it, Babs."

Babs nodded. She didn't catch the sarcasm. But she couldn't think very straight, just now. She was on the space platform, which was the second most glamorous spot in the universe. The most glamorous spot, of course, was the moon.

Cochrane hobbled ashore into the platform, having no weight whatever. He was able to move only by the curious sticky adhesion of his magnetic-soled slippers to the steel-floor-plates beneath him. Or—were they beneath?

There was a crew member walking upside down on a floor which ought to be a ceiling directly over Cochrane's head. He opened a door in a side-wall and went in, still upside down. Cochrane felt a sudden dizziness, at that.

But he went on, using hand-grips. Then he saw Dr. William Holden looking greenish and ill and trying sickishly to answer questions from West and Jamison and Bell, who had been plucked from their private lives just as Cochrane had and were now clamorously demanding of Bill Holden that he explain what had happened to them.

Cochrane snapped angrily:

"Leave the man alone! He's space-sick! If you get him too much upset this place will be a mess!"

Holden closed his eyes and said gratefully:

"Shoo them away, Jed, and then come back."

Cochrane waved his hands at them. They went away, stumbling and holding on to each other in the eerie dreamlikeness and nightmarish situation of no-weight-whatever. There were other passengers from the moon-rocket in this great central space of the platform. There was a fat woman looking indignantly at the picture of a weighing-scale painted on the wall. Somebody had painted it, with a dial-hand pointing to zero pounds. A sign said, *"Honest weight, no gravity."* There was the stewardess from the rocket, off duty here. She smoked a cigarette in the blast of an electric fan. There was a party of moon-tourists giggling foolishly and clutching at everything and buying souvenirs to mail back to Earth.

"All right, Bill," said Cochrane. "They're gone. Now tell me why all the not inconsiderable genius in the employ of Kursten, Kasten, Hopkins and Fallowe, in my person, has been mobilized and sent up to the moon?"

Bill Holden swallowed. He stood up with his eyes closed, holding onto a side-rail in the great central room of the platform.

"I have to keep my eyes shut," he explained, queasily. "It makes me ill to see people walking on side-walls and across ceilings."

A stout tourist was doing exactly that at the moment. If one could walk anywhere at all with magnetic-soled shoes, one could walk everywhere. The stout man did walk up the side-wall. He adventured onto the ceiling, where he was head-down to the balance of his party. He stood there looking up—down—at them, and he wore a

17

peculiarly astonished and half-frightened and wholly foolish grin. His wife squealed for him to come down: that she couldn't bear looking at him so.

"All right," said Cochrane. "You're keeping your eyes closed. But I'm supposed to take orders from you. What sort of orders are you going to give?"

"I'm not sure yet," said Holden thinly. "We are sent up here on a private job for Hopkins—one of your bosses. Hopkins has a daughter. She's married to a man named Dabney. He's neurotic. He's made a great scientific discovery and it isn't properly appreciated. So you and I and your team of tame scientists—we're on our way to the moon to save his reason."

"Why save his reason?" asked Cochrane cynically. "If it makes him happy to be a crackpot—"

"It doesn't," said Holden, with his eyes still closed. He gulped. "Your job and a large part of my practice depends on keeping him out of a looney-bin. It amounts to a public-relations job, a production, with me merely censoring aspects that might be bad for Dabney's psyche. Otherwise he'll be frustrated."

"Aren't we all?" demanded Cochrane. "Who in hades does he think he is? Most of us want appreciation, but we have to be glad when we do our work and get paid for it! We—"

Then he swore bitterly. He had been taken off the job he'd spent years learning to do acceptably, to phoney a personal satisfaction for the son-in-law of one of the partners of the firm he worked for. It was humiliation to be considered merely a lackey who could be ordered to perform personal services for his boss, without regard to the damage to the work he was really responsible for. It was even more humiliating to know he had to do it because he couldn't afford not to.

Babs appeared, obviously gloating over the mere fact that she was walking in magnetic-soled slippers on the steel decks of the space platform. Her eyes were very bright. She said:

"Mr. Cochrane, hadn't you better come look at Earth out of the quartz Earthside windows?"

"Why?" demanded Cochrane bitterly. "If it wasn't that I'd have to hold onto something with both hands, in order to do it, I'd be kicking myself. Why should I want to do tourist stuff?"

"So," said Babs, "so later on you can tell when a writer

or a scenic designer tries to put something over on you in a space platform show."

Cochrane grimaced.

"In theory, I should. But do you realize what all this is about? I just learned!" When Babs shook her head he said sardonically, "We are on the way to the moon to stage a private production out of sheer cruelty. We're hired to rob a happy man of the luxury of feeling sorry for himself. We're under Holden's orders to cure a man of being a crackpot!"

Babs hardly listened. She was too much filled with the zest of being where she'd never dared hope to be able to go.

"I wouldn't want to be cured of being a crackpot," protested Cochrane, "if only I could afford such a luxury! I'd—"

Babs said urgently:

"You'll have to hurry, really! They told me it starts in ten minutes, so I came to find you right away."

"What starts?"

"We're in eclipse now," explained Babs, starry-eyed. "We're in the Earth's shadow. In about five minutes we'll be coming out into sunlight again, and we'll see the new Earth!"

"Guarantee that it will be a new Earth," Cochrane said morosely, "and I'll come. I didn't do too well on the old one."

But he followed her in all the embarrassment of walking on magnetic-soled shoes in total absence of effective gravity. It was quite a job simply to start off. Without precaution, if he merely tried to march away from where he was, his feet would walk out from under him and he'd be left lying on his back in mid-air. Again, to stop without putting one foot out ahead for a prop would mean that after his feet paused, his body would continue onward and he would achieve a full-length face-down flop. And besides, one could not walk with a regular up-and-down motion, or in seconds he would find his feet churning emptiness in complete futility.

Cochrane tried to walk, and then irritably took a handrail and hauled himself along it, with his legs trailing behind him like the tail of a swimming mermaid. He thought of the simile and was not impressed by his own dignity.

Presently Babs halted herself in what was plainly a metal blister in the outer skin of the platform. There was a round quartz window, showing the inside of steel-plate windows beyond it. Babs pushed a button marked, *"Shutter,"* and the valves of steel drew back.

Cochrane blinked, lifted even out of his irritableness by the sight before him.

He saw the immensity of the heavens, studded with innumerable stars. Some were brighter than others, and they were of every imaginable color. Tiny glintings of lurid tint—through the Earth's atmosphere they would blend into an indefinite faint luminosity—appeared so close together that there seemed no possible interval. However tiny the appearance of a gap, one had but to look at it for an instant to perceive infinitesimal flecks of colored fire there, also.

Each tiniest glimmering was a sun. But that was not what made Cochrane catch his breath.

There was a monstrous space of nothingness immediately before his eyes. It was round and vast and near. It was black with the utter blackness of the Pit. It was Earth, seen from its eight-thousand-mile-wide shadow, unlighted even by the moon. There was no faintest relief from its absolute darkness. It was as if, in the midst of the splendor of the heavens, there was a chasm through which one glimpsed the unthinkable nothing from which creation was called in the beginning. Until one realized that this was simply the dark side of Earth, the spectacle was one of hair-raising horror.

After a moment Cochrane said with a carefully steadied voice:

"My most disparaging opinions of Earth were never as black as this!"

"Wait," said Babs confidently.

Cochrane waited. He had to hold carefully in his mind that this visible abyss, this enormity of purest dark, was not an opening into nothingness but was simply Earth at night as seen from space.

Then he saw a faint, faint arch of color forming at its edge. It spread swiftly. Immediately, it seemed, there was a pinkish glowing line among the multitudinous stars. It was red. It was very, very bright. It became a complete half-circle. It was the light of the sun refracted around the edge of the world.

Within minutes—it seemed in seconds—the line of light was a glory among the stars. And then, very swiftly, the blazing orb which was the sun appeared from behind Earth. It was intolerably bright, but it did not brighten

20

the firmament. It swam among all the myriads of myriads of suns, burning luridly and in a terrible silence, with visibly writhing prominences rising from the edge of its disk. Cochrane squinted at it with light-dazzled eyes.

Then Babs cried softly:

"Beautiful! Oh, beautiful!"

And Cochrane shielded his eyes and saw the world newborn before him. The arc of light became an arch and then a crescent, and swelled even as he looked. Dawn flowed below the space platform, and it seemed that seas and continents and clouds and beauty poured over the disk of darkness before him.

He stood there, staring, until the steel shutters slowly closed. Babs said in regret:

"You have to keep your hand on the button to keep the shutters open. Else the window might get pitted with dust."

Cochrane said cynically:

"And how much good will it have done me to see that, Babs? How can that be faked in a studio—and how much would a television screen show of it?"

He turned away. Then he added sourly:

"You stay and look if you like, Babs. I've already had my vanity smashed to little bits. If I look at that again I'll want to weep in pure frustration because I can't do anything even faintly as well worth watching. I prefer to cut down my notions of the cosmos to a tolerable size. But you go ahead and look!"

He went back to Holden. Holden was painfully dragging himself back into the rocket-ship. Cochrane went with him. They returned, weightless, to the admirably designed contour-chairs in which they had traveled to this place, and in which they would travel farther. Cochrane settled down to stare numbly at the wall above him. He had been humiliated enough by the actions of one of the heads of an advertising agency. He found himself resenting, even as he experienced, the humbling which had been imposed upon him by the cosmos itself.

Presently the other passengers returned, and the moon-ship was maneuvered out of the lock and to emptiness again, and again presently rockets roared and there was further feeling of intolerable weight. But it was not as bad as the takeoff from Earth.

There followed some ninety-six hours of pure tedium. After the first accelerating blasts, the rockets were silent.

21

There was no weight. There was nothing to hear except the droning murmur of unresting electric fans, stirring the air ceaselessly so that excess moisture from breathing could be extracted by the dehumidifiers. But for them—if the air had been left stagnant—the journey would have been insupportable.

There was nothing to see, because ports opening on outer space were not safe for passengers to look through. Mere humans, untrained to keep their minds on technical matters, could break down at the spectacle of the universe. There could be no activity.

Some of the passengers took dozy-pills. Cochrane did not. It was against the law for dozy-pills to produce a sensation of euphoria, of well-being. The law considered that pleasure might lead to addiction. But if a pill merely made a person drowsy, so that he dozed for hours halfway between sleeping and awake, no harm appeared to be done. Yet there were plenty of dozy-pill addicts. Many people were not especially anxious to feel good. They were quite satisfied not to feel anything at all.

Cochrane couldn't take that way of escape. He lay strapped in his chair and thought unhappily of many things. He came to feel unclean, as people used to feel when they traveled for days on end on railroad trains. There was no possibility of a bath. One could not even change clothes, because baggage went separately to the moon in a robot freight-rocket, which was faster and cheaper than a passenger transport, but would kill anybody who tried to ride it. Fifteen-and-twenty-gravity acceleration is economical of fuel, and six-gravity is not, but nobody can live through a twenty-gravity lift-off from Earth. So passengers stayed in the clothes in which they entered the ship, and the only possible concession to fastidiousness was the disposable underwear one could get and change to in the rest-rooms.

Babs Deane did not take dozy-pills either, but Cochrane knew better than to be more than remotely friendly with her outside of office hours. He did not want to give her any excuse to tell him anything for his own good. So he spoke pleasantly and kept company only with his own thoughts. But he did notice that she looked rapt and starry-eyed even through the long and dreary hours of free flight. She was mentally tracking the moonship through the void. She'd know when the continents of Earth were plain to see, and the tints of vegetation on the two hemispheres—northern and southern—and she'd know when Earth's ice-caps could be seen, and why.

The stewardess was not too much of a diversion. She was brisk and calm and soothing, but she became a trifle reluctant to draw too near the chairs in which her passengers rode. Presently Cochrane made deductions and maliciously devised a television commercial. In it, a moon-rocket stewardess, in uniform and looking fresh and charming, would say sweetly that she went without bathing for days at a time on moon-trips, and did not offend because she used whoosit's antistinkum. And then he thought pleasurably of the heads that would roll did such a commercial actually get on the air.

But he didn't make plans for the production-job he'd been sent to the moon to do. Psychiatry was specialized, these days, as physical medicine had been before it. An extremely expensive diagnostician had been sent to the moon to tap Dabney's reflexes, and he'd gravely diagnosed frustration and suggested young Dr. Holden for the curative treatment. Frustration was the typical neurosis of the rich, anyhow, and Bill Holden had specialized in its cure. His main reliance was on the making of a dramatic production centering about his patient, which was expensive enough and effective enough to have made him a quick reputation. But he couldn't tell Cochrane what was required of him. Not yet. He knew the disease but not the case. He'd have to see and know Dabney before he could make use of the extra-special production-crew his patient's father-in-law had provided from the staff of Kursten, Kasten, Hopkins and Fallowe.

Ninety-some hours after blast-off from the space platform, the rocket-ship turned end for end and began to blast to kill its velocity toward the moon. It began at half-gravity—the red glowing sign gave warning of it—and rose to one gravity and then to two. After days of no-weight, two gravities was punishing.

Cochrane thought to look at Babs. She was rapt, lost in picturings of what must be outside the ship, which she could not see. She'd be imagining what the television screens had shown often enough, from film-tapes. The great pock-marked face of Luna, with its ring-mountains in incredible numbers and complexity, and the vast open "seas" which were solidified oceans of lava, would be clear to her mind's eye. She would be imagining the gradual changes of the moon's face with nearness, when the colorings appear.

23

From a distance all the moon seems tan or sandy in tint. When one comes closer, there are tawny reds and slate-colors in the mountain-cliffs, and even blues and yellows, and everywhere there is the ashy, whitish-tan color of the moondust.

Glancing at her, absorbed in her satisfaction, Cochrane suspected that with only half an excuse she would explain to him how the several hundreds of degrees difference in the surface-temperature of the moon between midnight and noon made rocks split and re-split and fracture so that stuff as fine as talcum powder covered every space not too sharply tilted for it to rest on.

The feeling of deceleration increased. For part of a second they had the sensation of three gravities.

Then there was a curious, yielding jar—really very slight —and then the feeling of excess weight ended altogether. But not the feeling of weight. They still had weight. It was constant. It was steady. But it was very slight.

They were on the moon, but Cochrane felt no elation. In the tedious hours from the space platform he'd thought too much. He was actually aware of the humiliations and frustrations most men had to conceal from themselves because they couldn't afford expensive psychiatric treatments. Frustration was the disease of all humanity, these days. And there was nothing that could be done about it. Nothing! It simply wasn't possible to rebel, and rebellion is the process by which humiliation and frustration is cured. But one could not rebel against the plain fact that Earth had more people on it than one planet could support.

Merely arriving at the moon did not seem an especially useful achievement, either to Cochrane or to humanity at large.

Things looked bad.

CHAPTER TWO

COCHRANE STOOD WHEN THE STEWARDESS' VOICE AU-
thorized the action. With sardonic docility he unfastened his
safety-belt and stepped out into the spiral, descending aisle.
It seemed strange to have weight again, even as little as this.
Cochrane weighed, on the moon, just one-sixth of what he
would weigh on Earth. Here he would tip a spring-scale at
just about twenty-seven pounds. By flexing his toes, he
could jump. Absurdly, he did. And he rose very slowly, and
hovered—feeling singularly foolish—and descended with a
vast deliberation. He landed on the ramp again feeling
absurd indeed. He saw Babs grinning at him.

"I think," said Cochrane, "I'll have to take up toe-danc-
ing."

She laughed. Then there were clankings, and something
fastened itself outside, and after a moment the entrance-
door of the moonship opened.

They went down the ramp to board the moonjeep,
holding onto the hand-rail and helping each other. The
tourist giggled foolishly. They went out the thick doorway
and found themselves in an enclosure very much like the
interior of a rather small submarine. But it did have
shielded windows—ports—and Babs instantly pulled herself into a seat beside one and feasted her eyes. She saw
the jagged peaks nearby and the crenelated ring-mountain
wall, miles off to one side, and the smooth frozen lava of
the "sea." Across that dusty surface the horizon was remarkably near, and Cochrane remembered vaguely that
the moon was only one-fourth the size of Earth, so its
horizon would naturally be nearer. He glanced at the stars
that shone even through the glass that denatured the sunshine. And then he looked for Holden.

The psychiatrist looked puffy and sleepy and haggard
and disheveled. When a person does have space-sickness,

even a little weight relieves the symptoms, but the consequences last for days.

"Don't worry!" he said sourly when he saw Cochrane's eyes upon him. "I won't waste any time! I'll find my man and get to work at once. Just let me get back to Earth . . ."

There were more clankings—the jeep-bus sealing off from the rocket. Then the vehicle stirred. The landscape outside began to move.

They saw Lunar City as they approached it. It was five giant dust-heaps, from five hundred-odd feet in height down to three. There were airlocks at their bases and dust-covered tunnels connecting them, and radar-bowls about their sides. But they were dust-heaps. Which was completely reasonable. There is no air on the moon. By day the sun shines down with absolute ferocity. It heats everything as with a furnace-flame. At night all heat radiates away to empty space, and the ground-temperature drops well below that of liquid air. So Lunar City was a group of domes which were essentially half-balloons—hemispheres of plastic brought from Earth and inflated and covered with dust. With airlocks to permit entrance and exit, they were inhabitable. They needed no framework to support them because there were no stormwinds or earthquakes to put stresses on them. They needed neither heating nor cooling equipment. They were buried under forty feet of moon-dust, with vacuum between the dust-grains. Lunar City was not beautiful, but human beings could live in it.

The jeep-bus carried them a bare half mile, and they alighted inside a lock, and another door and another opened and closed, and they emerged into a scene which no amount of television film-tape could really portray.

The main dome was a thousand feet across and half as high. There were green plants growing in tubs and pots. And the air was fresh! It smelled strange. There could be no vegetation on the rocket and it seemed new and blissful to breathe really freshened air after days of the canned variety. But this freshness made Cochrane realize that he'd feel better for a bath.

He took a shower in his hotel room. The room was very much like one on Earth, except that it had no windows. But the shower was strange. The sprays were tiny. Cochrane felt as if he were being sprayed by atomizers rather than shower-nozzles until he noticed that water ran off him very slowly and realized that a normal shower would have been overwhelming. He scooped up a handful of water and let it drop. It took a full second to fall two and a half feet.

It was unsettling, but fresh clothing from his waiting baggage made him feel better. He went to the lounge of the hotel, and it was not a lounge, and the hotel was not a hotel. Everything in the dome was indoors in the sense that it was under a globular ceiling fifty stories high. But everything was also out-doors in the sense of bright light and growing trees and bushes and shrubs.

He found Babs freshly garmented and waiting for him. She said in businesslike tones:

"Mr. Cochrane, I asked at the desk. Doctor Holden has gone to consult Mr. Dabney. He asked that we stay within call. I've sent word to Mr. West and Mr. Jamison and Mr. Bell."

Cochrane approved of her secretarial efficiency.

"Then we'll sit somewhere and wait. Since this isn't an office, we'll find some refreshment."

They asked for a table and got one near the swimming pool. And Babs wore her office manner, all crispness and business, until they were seated. But this swimming pool was not like a pool on Earth. The water was deeply sunk beneath the pool's rim, and great waves surged back and forth. The swimmers—.

Babs gasped. A man stood on a board quite thirty feet above the water. He prepared to dive.

"That's Johnny Simms!" she said, awed.

"Who's he?"

"The playboy," said Babs, staring. "He's a psychopathic personality and his family has millions. They keep him up here out of trouble. He's married."

"Too bad—if he has millions," said Cochrane.

"I wouldn't marry a man with a psychopathic personality!" protested Babs.

"Keep away from people in the advertising business, then," Cochrane told her.

Johnny Simms did not jounce up and down on the diving board to start. He simply leaped upward, and went ceilingward for easily fifteen feet, and hung stationary for a full breath, and then began to descend in literal slow motion. He fell only two and a half feet the first second, and five feet more the one after, and twelve and a half after that . . . It took him over four seconds to drop forty-five feet into the water, and the splash that arose when he struck

27

the surface rose four yards and subsided with a lunatic deliberation.

Watching, Babs could not keep her businesslike demeanor. She was bursting with the joyous knowledge that she was on the moon, seeing the impossible and looking at fame.

They sipped at drinks—but the liquid rose much too swiftly in the straws—and Cochrane reflected that the drink in Babs' glass would cost Dabney's father-in-law as much as Babs earned in a week back home, and his own was costing no less.

Presently a written note came from Holden:

"Jed: send West and Jamison right away to Dabney's lunar laboratory to get details of discovery from man named Jones. Get moon-jeep and driver from hotel. I will want you in an hour.—Bill."

"I'll be back," said Cochrane. "Wait."

He left the table and found West and Jamison in Bell's room, all three in conference over a bottle. West and Jamison were Cochrane's scientific team for the yet unformulated task he was to perform. West was the popularizing specialist. He could make a television audience believe that it understood all the seven dimensions required for some branches of wave-mechanics theory. His explanations did not stick, of course. One didn't remember them. But they were singularly convincing in cultural episodes on television productions. Jamison was the prophecy expert. He could extrapolate anything into anything else, and make you believe that a one-week drop in the birthrate on Kamchatka was the beginning of a trend that would leave the Earth depopulated in exactly four hundred and seventy-three years. They were good men for a television producer to have on call. Now, instructed, they went out to be briefed by somebody who undoubtedly knew more than both of them put together, but whom they would regard with tolerant suspicion.

Bell, left behind, said cagily:

"This script I've got to do, now—Will that laboratory be the set? Where is it? In the dome?"

"It's not in the dome," Cochrane told him. "West and Jamison took a moon-jeep to get to it. I don't know what the set will be. I don't know anything, yet. I'm waiting to be told about the job, myself."

28

"If I've got to cook up a story-line," observed Bell, "I have to know the set. Who'll act? You know how amateurs can ham up any script! How about a part for Babs? Nice kid!"

Cochrane found himself annoyed, without knowing why.

"We just have to wait until we know what our job is," he said curtly, and turned to go.

Bell said:

"One more thing. If you're planning to use a news cameraman up here—don't! I used to be a cameraman before I got crazy and started to write. Let me do the camera-work. I've got a better idea of using a camera to tell a story now, than——"

"Hold it," said Cochrane. "We're not up here to film-tape a show. Our job is psychiatry—craziness."

To a self-respecting producer, a psychiatric production would seem craziness. A script-writer might have trouble writing out a psychiatrist's prescription, or he might not. But producing it would be out of all rationality! No camera, the patient would be the star, and most lines would be ad libbed. Cochrane viewed such a production with extreme distaste. But of course, if a man wanted only to be famous, it might be handled as a straight public-relations job. In any case, though, it would amount to flattery in three dimensions and Cochrane would rather have no part in it. But he had to arrange the whole thing.

He went back to the table and rejoined Babs. She confided that she'd been talking to Johnny Simms' wife. She was nice! But homesick. Cochrane sat down and thought morbid thoughts. Then he realized that he was irritated because Babs didn't notice. He finished his drink and ordered another.

Half an hour later, Holden found them. He had in tow a sad-looking youngish man with a remarkably narrow forehead and an expression of deep anxiety. Cochrane winced. A neurotic type if there ever was one!

"Jed," said Holden heartily, "here's Mr. Dabney. Mr. Dabney, Jed Cochrane is here as a specialist in public-relations set-ups. He'll take charge of this affair. Your father-in-law sent him up here to see that you are done justice to!"

Dabney seemed to think earnestly before he spoke.

"It is not for myself," he explained in an anxious tone. "It is my work! That is important! After all, this is a fundamental scientific discovery! But nobody pays any attention! It is extremely important! Extremely! Science itself is held back by the lack of attention paid to my discovery!"

"Which," Holden assured him, "is about to be changed. It's a matter of public relations. Jed's a specialist. He'll take over."

The sad-faced young man held up his hand for attention. He thought. Visibly. Then he said worriedly:

"I would take you over to my laboratory, but I promised my wife I would call her in half an hour from now. Johnny Simms' wife just reminded me. My wife is back on Earth. So you will have to go to the laboratory without me and have Mr. Jones show you the proof of my work. A very intelligent man, Jones—in a subordinate way, of course. Yes. I will get you a jeep and you can go there at once, and when you come back you can tell me what you plan. But you understand that it is not for myself that I want credit! It is my discovery! It is terribly important! It is vital! It must not be overlooked!"

Holden escorted him away, while Cochrane carefully controlled his features. After a few moments Holden came back, his face sagging.

"This is your drink, Jed?" he asked dispiritedly. "I need it!" He picked up the glass and emptied it. "The history of that case would be interesting, if one could really get to the bottom of it! Come along!" His tone was dreariness itself. "I've got a jeep waiting for us."

Babs stood up, her eyes shining.

"May I come, Mr. Cochrane?"

Cochrane waved her along. Holden tried to stalk gloomily, but nobody can stalk in one-sixth gravity. He reeled, and then depressedly accommodated himself to conditions on the moon.

There was an airlock with a smaller edition of the moon-jeep that had brought them from the ship to the city. It was a brightly-polished metal body, raised some ten feet off the ground on outrageously large wheels. It was very similar to the straddle-trucks used in lumber-yards on Earth. It would straddle boulders in its path. It could go anywhere in spite of dust and detritus, and its metal body was air-tight and held air for breathing, even out on the moon's surface.

They climbed in. There was the sound of pumping, which grew fainter. The outer lock-door opened. The moon-jeep rolled outside.

Babs stared with passionate rapture out of a shielded

30

port. There were impossibly jagged stones, preposterously steep cliffs. There had been no weather to remove the sharp edge of anything in a hundred million years. The awkward-seeming vehicle trundled over the lava sea toward the rampart of mighty mountains towering over Lunar City. It reached a steep ascent. It climbed. And the way was remarkably rough and the vehicle springless, but it was nevertheless a cushioned ride. A bump cannot be harsh in light gravity. The vehicle rode as if on wings.

"All right," said Cochrane. "Tell me the worst. What's the trouble with him? Is he the result of six generations of keeping the money in the family? Or is he a freak?"

Holden groaned a little.

"He's practically a stock model of a rich young man without brains enough for a job in the family firm, and too much money for anything else. Fortunately for his family, he didn't react like Johnny Simms—though they're good friends. A hundred years ago, Dabney'd have gone in for the arts. But it's hard to fool yourself that way now. Fifty years ago he'd have gone in for left-wing sociology. But we really are doing the best that can be done with too many people and not enough world. So he went in for science. It's non-competitive. Incapacity doesn't show up. But he has stumbled on something. It sounds really important. It must have been an accident! The only trouble is that it doesn't mean a thing! Yet because he's accomplished more than he ever expected to, he's frustrated because it's not appreciated! What a joke!"

Cochrane said cynically:

"You paint a dark picture, Bill. Are you trying to make this thing into a challenge?"

"You can't make a man famous for discovering something that doesn't matter," said Holden hopelessly. "And this is that!"

"Nothing's impossible to public relations if you spend enough money," Cochrane assured him. "What's this useless triumph of his?"

The jeep bounced over a small cliff and fell gently for half a second and rolled on. Babs beamed.

"He's found," said Holden discouragedly, "a way to send messages faster than light. It's a detour around Einstein's stuff—not denying it, but evading it. Right now it takes not quite two seconds for a message to go from the moon to Earth. That's at the speed of light. Dabney has proof—we'll see it—that he can cut that down some ninety-five per

31

cent. Only it can't be used for Earth-moon communication, because both ends have to be in a vacuum. It could be used to the space platform, but—what's the difference? It's a real discovery for which there's no possible use. There's no place to send messages to!"

Cochrane's eyes grew bright and hard. There were some three thousand million suns in the immediate locality of Earth—and more only a relatively short distance way—and it had not mattered to anybody. The situation did not seem likely to change. But— The moon-jeep climbed and climbed. It was a mile above the bay of the lava sea and the dust-heaps that were a city. It looked like ten miles, because of the curve of the horizon. The mountains all about looked like a madman's dream.

"But he wants appreciation!" said Holden angrily. "People on Earth almost trampling on each other for lack of room, and people like me trying to keep them sane when they've every reason for despair—and he wants appreciation!"

Cochrane grinned. He whistled softly.

"Never underestimate a genius, Bill," he said kindly. "I refer modestly to myself. In two weeks your patient—I'll guarantee it—will be acclaimed the hope, the blessing, the greatest man in all the history of humanity! It'll be phoney, of course, but we'll have Marilyn Winters—Little Aphrodite herself—making passes at him in hopes of a publicity break! It's a natural!"

"How'll you do it?" demanded Holden.

The moon-jeep turned in its crazy, bumping progress. A flat area had been blasted in rock which had been unchanged since the beginning of time. Here there was a human structure. Typically, it was a dust-heap leaning against a cliff. There was an airlock and another jeep waited outside, and there were eccentric metal devices on the flat space, shielded from direct sunshine and with cables running to them from the airlock door.

"How?" repeated Cochrane. "I'll get the details here. Let's go! How do we manage?"

It was a matter, he discovered, of vacuum-suits, and they were tricky to get into and felt horrible when one was in. Struggling, Cochrane thought to say:

"You can wait here in the jeep, Babs—"

But she was already climbing into a suit very much oversized for her, with the look of high excitement that Cochrane had forgotten anybody could wear.

They got out of a tiny airlock that held just one person at a time. They started for the laboratory. And suddenly Cochrane saw Babs staring upward through the dark, almost-opaque glass that a space-suit-helmet needs in the moon's daytime if its occupant isn't to be fried by sunlight. Cochrane automatically glanced up too.

He saw Earth. It hung almost in mid-sky. It was huge. It was gigantic. It was colossal. It was four times the diameter of the moon as seen from Earth, and it covered sixteen times as much of the sky. Its continents were plain to see, and its seas, and the ice-caps at its poles gleamed whitely, and over all of it there was a faintly bluish haze which was like a glamour; a fey and eerie veiling which made Earth a sight to draw at one's heart-strings.

Behind it and all about it there was the background of space, so thickly jeweled with stars that there seemed no room for another tiny gem.

Cochrane looked. He said nothing. Holden stumbled on to the airlock. He remembered to hold the door open for Babs.

And then there was the interior of the laboratory. It was not wholly familiar even to Cochrane, who had used sets on the Dikkipatti Hour of most of the locations in which human dramas can unfold. This was a physics laboratory, pure and simple. The air smelled of ozone and spilled acid and oil and food and tobacco-smoke and other items. West and Jamison were already here, their space-suits removed. They sat before beer at a table with innumerable diagrams scattered about. There was a deep-browed man rather impatiently turning to face his new visitors.

Holden clumsily unfastened the face-plate of his helmet and gloomily explained his mission. He introduced Cochrane and Babs, verifying in the process that the dark man was the Jones he had come to see. A physics laboratory high in the fastnesses of the Lunar Appenines is an odd place for a psychiatrist to introduce himself on professional business. But Holden only explained unhappily that Dabney had sent them to learn about his discovery and arrange for a public-relations job to make it known.

Cochrane saw Jones' expression flicker sarcastically just once during Holden's explanation. Otherwise he was poker-faced.

"I was explaining the discovery to these two," he observed.

"Shoot it," said Cochrane to West. It was reasonable to

33

ask West for an explanation, because he would translate everything into televisable terms.

West said briskly—exactly as if before a television camera—that Mr. Dabney had started from the well-known fact that the properties of space are modified by energy fields. Magnetic and gravitational and electrostatic fields rotate polarized light or bend light or do this or that as the case may be. But all previous modifications of the constants of space had been in essentially spherical fields. All previous fields had extended in all directions, increasing in intensity as the square of the distance . . .

"Cut," said Cochrane.

West automatically abandoned his professional delivery. He placidly re-addressed himself to his beer.

"How about it, Jones?" asked Cochrane. "Dabney's got a variation? What is it?"

"It's a field of force that doesn't spread out. You set up two plates and establish this field between them," said Jones curtly. "It's circularly polarized and it doesn't expand. It's like a searchlight beam or a microwave beam, and it stays the same size like a pipe. In that field—or pipe—radiation travels faster than it does outside. The properties of space are changed between the plates. Therefore the speed of all radiation. That's all."

Cochrane meditatively seated himself. He approved of this Jones, whose eyebrows practically met in the middle of his forehead. He was not more polite than politeness required. He did not express employee-like rapture at the mention of his employer's name.

"But what can be done with it?" asked Cochrane practically.

"Nothing," said Jones succinctly. "It changes the properties of space, but that's all. Can you think of any use for a faster-than-light radiation-pipe? I can't."

Cochrane cocked an eye at Jamison, who could extrapolate at the drop of an equation. But Jamison shook his head.

"Communication between planets," he said morosely, "when we get to them. Chats between sweethearts on Earth and Pluto. Broadcasts to the stars when we find that another one's set up a similar plate and is ready to chat with us. There's nothing else."

Cochrane waved his hand. It is good policy to put a specialist in his place, occasionally.

"Demonstration?" he asked Jones.

34

"There are plates across the crater out yonder," said Jones without emotion. "Twenty miles clear reach. I can send a message across and get it relayed twice and back through two angles in about five per cent of the time radiation ought to take."

Cochrane said with benign cynicism:

"Jamison, you work by guessing where you can go. Jones works by guessing where he is. But this is a public relations job. I don't know where we are or where we can go, but I know where we want to take this thing."

Jones looked at him. Not hostilely, but with the detached interest of a man accustomed to nearly exact science, when he watches somebody work in one of the least precise of them all.

Holden said:

"You mean you've worked out some sort of production."

"No production," said Cochrane blandly. "It isn't necessary. A straight public-relations set-up. We concoct a story and then let it leak out. We make it so good that even the people who don't believe it can't help spreading it." He nodded at Jamison. "Right now, Jamison, we want a theory that the sending of radiation at twenty times the speed of light means that there is a way to send matter faster than light—as soon as we work it out. It means that the inertia-mass which increases with speed—Einstein's stuff—is not a property of matter, but of space, just as the air-resistance that increases when an airplane goes faster is a property of air and not of the plane. Maybe we need to work out a theory that all inertia is a property of space. We'll see if we need that. But anyhow, just as a plane can go faster in thin air, so matter—any matter—will move faster in this field as soon as we get the trick of it. You see?"

Holden shook his head.

"What's that got in it to make Dabney famous?" he asked.

"Jamison will extrapolate from there," Cochrane assured him. "Go ahead, Jamison. You're on."

Jamison said promptly, with the hypnotic smoothness of the practiced professional:

"When this development has been completed, not only will messages be sent at multiples of the speed of light, but matter! Ships! The barrier to the high destiny of mankind; the limitation of our race to a single planet of a minor sun

35

—these handicaps crash and will shatter as the great minds of humanity bend their efforts to make the Dabney faster-than-light principle the operative principle of our ships. There are thousands of millions of suns in our galaxy, and not less than one in three has planets, and among these myriads of unknown worlds there will be thousands with seas and land and clouds and continents, fit for men to enter upon, there to rear their cities. There will be starships roaming distant sun-clusters, and landing on planets in the Milky Way. We ourselves will see freight-lines to Rigel and Arcturus, and journey on passenger-liners singing through the void to Andromeda and Aldebaran! Dabney has made the first breach in the barrier to the illimitable greatness of humanity!"

Then he stopped and said professionally:

"I can polish that up a bit, of course. All right?"

"Fair," conceded Cochrane. He turned to Holden. "How about a public-relations job on that order? Won't that sort of publicity meet the requirements? Will your patient be satisfied with that grade of appreciation?"

Holden drew a deep breath. He said unsteadily:

"As a neurotic personality, he won't require that it be true. All he'll want is the seeming. But—Jed, could it be really true? Could it?"

Cochrane laughed unpleasantly. He did not admire himself. His laughter showed it.

"What do you want?" he demanded. "You got me a job I didn't want. You shoved it down my throat! Now there's the way to get it done! What more can you ask?"

Holden winced. Then he said heavily:

"I'd like for it to be true."

Jones moved suddenly. He said in an oddly surprised voice:

"D'you know, it can be! I didn't realize! It can be true! I can make a ship go faster than light!"

Cochrane said with exquisite irony:

"Thanks, but we don't need it. We aren't getting paid for that! All we need is a modicum of appreciation for a neurotic son-in-law of a partner of Kursten, Kasten, Hopkins and Fallowe! A public-relations job is all that's required. You give West the theory, and Jamison will do the prophecy, and Bell will write it out."

Jones said calmly:

"I will like hell! Look! I discovered this faster-than-light field in the first place! I sold it to Dabney because he

36

wanted to be famous! I got my pay and he can keep it! But if he can't understand it himself, even to lecture about it ... Do you think I'm going to throw in some extra stuff I noticed, that I can fit into that theory but nobody else can—Do you think I'm going to give him starships as a bonus?"

Holden said, nodding, with his lips twisted:

"I should have figured that! He bought his great discovery from you, eh? And that's what he gets frustrated about!"

Cochrane snapped:

"I thought you psychiatrists knew the facts of life, Bill! Dabney's not unusual in my business! He's almost a typical sponsor!"

"When you ask me to throw away starships," said Jones coldly, "for a publicity feature, I don't play. I won't take the credit for the field away from Dabney. I sold him that with my eyes open. But starships are more important than a fool's hankering to be famous! He'd never try it! He'd be afraid it wouldn't work! I don't play!"

Holden said stridently:

"I don't give a damn about any deal you made with Dabney! But if you can get us to the stars—all us humans who need it—you've got to!"

Jones said, again calmly:

"I'm willing. Make me an offer—not cash, but a chance to do something real—not just a trick for a neurotic's ego!"

Cochrane grinned at him very peculiarly.

"I like your approach. You've got illusions. They're nice things to have. I wouldn't mind having some myself. Bill," he said to Dr. William Holden, "how much nerve has Dabney?"

"Speaking unprofessionally," said Holden, "he's a worm with wants. He hasn't anything but cravings. Why?"

Cochrane grinned again, his head cocked on one side.

"He wouldn't take part in an enterprise to reach the stars, would he?" When Holden shook his head, Cochrane said zestfully, "I'd guess that the peak of his ambition would be to have the credit for it if it worked, but he wouldn't risk being associated with it until it had worked! Right?"

"Right," said Holden. "I said he was a worm. What're you driving at?"

"I'm outlining what you're twisting my arm to make me do," said Cochrane, "in case you haven't noticed. Bill, if

37

Jones can really make a ship go faster than light——"

"I can," repeated Jones. "I simply didn't think of the thing in connection with travel. I only thought of it for signalling."

"Then," said Cochrane, "I'm literally forced, for Dabney's sake, to do something that he'd scream shrilly at if he heard about it. We're going to have a party, Bill! A party after your and my and Jones' hearts!"

"What do you mean?" demanded Holden.

"We make a production after all," said Cochrane, grinning. "We are going to take Dabney's discovery—the one he bought publicity rights to—very seriously indeed. I'm going to get him acclaim. First we break a story of what Dabney's field means for the future of mankind—and then we prove it! We take a journey to the stars! Want to make your reservations now?"

"You mean," said West incredulously, "a genuine trip? Why?"

Cochrane snapped at him suddenly.

"Because I can't kid myself any more," he rasped. "I've found out how little I count in the world and the estimation of Kursten, Kasten, Hopkins and Fallowe! I've found out I'm only a little man when I thought I was a big one, and I won't take it! Now I've got an excuse to try to be a big man! That's reason enough, isn't it?"

Then he glared around the small laboratory under the dust-heap. He was irritated because he did not feel splendid emotions after making a resolution and a plan which ought to go down in history—if it worked. He wasn't uplifted. He wasn't aware of any particular feeling of being the instrument of destiny or anything else. He simply felt peevish and annoyed and obstinate about trying the impossible trick.

It annoyed him additionally, perhaps, to see the expression of starry-eyed admiration on Babs' face as she looked at him across the untidy laboratory table, cluttered up with beer-cans.

CHAPTER THREE

IT IS A MATTER OF RECORD THAT THE AMERICAN CONtinents were discovered because ice-boxes were unknown in the fifteenth century. There being no refrigeration, meat did not keep. But meat was not too easy to come by, so it had to be eaten, even when it stank. Therefore it was a noble enterprise, and to the glory of the kingdoms of Castile and Aragon, to put up the financial backing for even a crackpot who might get spices cheaper and thereby make the consumption of slightly spoiled meat less unpleasant. Which was why Columbus got three ships and crews of jailbirds for them from a government still busy trying to drive the Moors out of the last corner of Spain.

This was a precedent for the matter on hand now. Cochrane happened to know the details about Columbus because he'd checked over the research when he did a show on the Dikkipatti Hour dealing with him. There were more precedents. The elaborate bargain by which Columbus was to be made hereditary High Admiral of the Western Oceans, with a bite of all revenue obtained by the passage he was to discover—he had to hold out for such terms to make the package he was selling look attractive. Nobody buys anything that is underpriced too much. It looks phoney. So Cochrane made his preliminaries rather more impressive than they need have been from a strictly practical point of view, in order to make the enterprise practical from a financial aspect.

There was another precedent he did not intend to follow. Columbus did not know where he was going when he set sail, he did not know where he was when he arrived at the end of his voyage, and he didn't know where he'd been when he got back. Cochrane expected to improve on the achievement of the earlier explorer's doings in these respects.

He commandeered the legal department of Kursten,

Kasten, Hopkins and Fallowe to set up the enterprise with strict legality and discretion. There came into being a corporation called "Spaceways, Inc.," which could not possibly be considered phoney from any inspection of its charter. Expert legal advice arranged that its actual stockholders should appear to be untraceable. Deft manipulation contrived that though its stock was legally vested in Cochrane and Holden and Jones—Cochrane negligently threw in Jones as a convenient name to use—and they were officially the owners of nearly all the stock, nobody who checked up would believe they were anything but dummies. Stockholdings in West's, and Jamison's and Bell's names would look like smaller holdings held for other than the main entrepreneurs. But these stockholders were not only the legal owners of record—they were the true owners. Kursten, Kasten, Hopkins and Fallowe wanted no actual part of Spaceways. They considered the enterprise merely a psychiatric treatment for a neurotic son-in-law. Which, of course, it was. So Spaceways, Inc., quite honestly and validly belonged to the people who would cure Dabney of his frustration—and nobody at all believed that it would ever do anything else. Not anybody but those six owners, anyhow. And as it turned out, not all of them.

The psychiatric treatment began with an innocent-seeming news-item from Lunar City saying that Dabney, the so-and-so scientist, had consented to act as consulting physicist to Spaceways, Inc., for the practical application of his recent discovery of a way to send messages faster than light.

This was news simply because it came from the moon. It got fairly wide distribution, but no emphasis.

Then the publicity campaign broke. On orders from Cochrane, Jamison the extrapolating genius got slightly plastered, in company with the two news-association reporters in Lunar City. He confided that Spaceways, Inc., had been organized and was backed to develop the Dabney faster-than-light-signalling field into a faster-than-light-travel field. The news men pumped him of all his extrapolations. Cynically, they checked to see who might be preparing to unload stock. They found no preparations for stock-sales. No registration of the company for raising funds. It wasn't going to the public for money. It wasn't selling anybody anything. Then Cochrane refused to see any reporters at all, everybody connected with the enterprise shut up tighter than a clam, and Jamison vanished into a hotel room where he was kept occupied with beverages and food at Dabney's father-in-law's expense. None of this was standard for a phoney promotion deal.

The news story exploded. Let loose on an overcrowded planet which had lost all hope of relief after fifty years in which only the moon had been colonized—and its colony had a population in the hundreds, only—the idea of faster-than-light travel was the one impossible dream that everybody wanted to believe in. The story spread in a manner that could only be described as chain-reaction in character. And of course Dabney—as the scientist responsible for the new hope—became known to all peoples.

The experts of Kursten, Kasten, Hopkins and Fallowe checked on the publicity given to Dabney. Strict advertising agency accounting figured that to date the cost-per-customer-mention of Dabney and his discovery were the lowest in the history of advertising. Surveys disclosed that within three Earth-days less than 3.5 of every hundred interviews questioned were completely ignorant of Dabney and the prospect of travel to the stars through his discovery. More people knew Dabney's name than knew the name of the President of the United States!

That was only the beginning. The leading popular-science show jumped eight points in audience-rating. It actually reached top-twenty rating when it assigned a regular five-minute period to the Dabney Field and its possibilities in human terms. On the sixth day after Jamison's calculated indiscretion, the public consciousness was literally saturated with the idea of faster-than-light transportation. Dabney was mentioned in every interview of every stuffed shirt, he was referred to on every comedy show (three separate jokes had been invented, which were developed into one thousand eight hundred switcheroos, most of them only imperceptibly different from the original trio) and even Marilyn Winters—Little Aphrodite Herself—was demanding a faster-than-light-travel sequence in her next television show.

On the seventh day Bill Holden came into the office where Cochrane worked feverishly.

"Doctor Cochrane," said Holden, "a word with you!"

"Doctor?" asked Cochrane.

"Doctor!" repeated Holden. "I've just been interviewing my patient. You're good. My patient is adjusted."

Cochrane raised his eyebrows.

"He's famous," said Holden grimly. "He now considers that everybody in the world knows that he is a great scientist. He is appreciated. He is happily making plans to go back to Earth and address a few learned societies and let people admire him. He can now spend the rest of his life being the man who discovered the principle by which faster-than-light-travel will some day be achieved. Even when the furor dies down, he will have been a great man —and he will stay a great man in his own estimation. In short, he's cured."

Cochrane grinned.

"Then I'm fired?"

"We are," said Holden. "There are professional ethics even among psychiatrists, Jed. I have to admit that the guy now has a permanent adjustment to reality. He has been recognized as a great scientist. He is no longer frustrated."

Cochrane leaned back in his chair.

"That may be good medical ethics," he observed, "but it's lousy business practice, Bill. You say he's adjusted to reality. That means that he will now have a socially acceptable reaction to anything that's likely to happen to him."

Holden nodded.

"A well-adjusted person does. Dabney's the same person. He's the same fool. But he'll get along all right. A psychiatrist can't change a personality! All he can do is make it adjust to the world about so the guy doesn't have to be tucked away in a straight-jacket. In that sense, Dabney is adjusted."

"You've played a dirty trick on him," said Cochrane. "You've stabilized him, and that's the rottenest trick anybody can play on anybody! You've put him into a sort of moral deep-freeze. It's a dirty trick, Bill!"

"Look who's talking!" said Holden wearily. "I suppose the advertising business is altruistic and unmercenary?"

"The devil, no!" said Cochrane indignantly. "We serve a useful purpose! We tell people that they smell bad, and so give them an alibi for the unpopularity their stupidity has produced. But then we tell them to use so-and-so's breath sweetener or whosit's non-immunizing deodorant they'll immediately become the life of every party they attend! It's a lie, of course, but it's a dynamic lie! It gives the frustrated individual something to do! It sells him hope and therefore activity—and inactivity is a sort of death!"

42

Holden looked at Cochrane with a dreary disinterest.

"You're adjusted, Jed! But do you really believe that stuff?"

Cochrane grinned again.

"Only on Tuesdays and Fridays. It's about two-sevenths true. But it does have that much truth in it! Nobody ever gets anything done while they merely make socially acceptable responses to the things that happen to them! Take Dabney himself! We've got a hell of a thing coming along now just because he wouldn't make the socially acceptable response to having a rich wife and no brains. He rebelled. So mankind will start moving to the stars!"

"You still believe it?"

Cochrane grimaced.

"Yesterday morning I sweated blood in a space-suit out in the crater beyond Jones' laboratory. He tried his trick. He had a small signal-rocket mounted on the far side of that crater,—twenty-some miles. It was in front of the field-plate that established the Dabney field across the crater to another plate near us. Jones turned on the field. He ignited the rocket by remote control. I was watching with a telescope. I gave him the word to fire . . . How long do you think it took that rocket to cross the crater in that field that works like a pipe? It smashed into the plate at the lab!"

Holden shook his head.

"It took slightly," said Cochrane, "slightly under three-fifths of a second."

Holden blinked. Cochrane said:

"A signal-rocket has an acceleration of about six hundred feet per second, level flight, no gravity component, mass acceleration only. It should have taken a hundred seconds plus to cross that crater—over twenty miles. It shouldn't have stayed on course. It did stay on course, inside the field. It did take under three-fifths of a second. The gadget works!"

Holden drew a deep breath.

"So now you need more money and you want me not to discharge my patient as cured."

"Not a bit of it!" snapped Cochrane. "I don't want him as a patient! I'm only willing to accept him as a customer! But if he wants fame, I'll sell it to him. Not as something to lean his fragile psyche on, but something to wallow in! Do you think he could ever get too famous for his own satisfaction?"

"Of course not," said Holden. "He's the same fool."

"Then we're in business," Cochrane told him. "Not that I couldn't peddle my fish elsewhere. I'm going to! But I'll give him old-customer preference. I'll want him out at the distress-torp tests this afternoon. They'll be public."

"This afternoon?" asked Holden. "Distress-torp?"

A lunar day is two Earth-weeks long. A lunar night is equally long-drawn-out. Cochrane said impatiently:

"I got out of bed four hours ago. To me that's morning. I'll eat lunch in an hour. That's noon. Say, three hours from now, whatever o'clock it is lunar time."

Holden glanced at his watch and made computations. He said:

"That'll be half-past two hundred and three o'clock, if you're curious. But what's a distress-torp?"

"Shoo!" said Cochrane. "I'll send Babs to find you and load you on the jeep. You'll see then. Now I'm busy!"

Holden shrugged and went away, and Cochrane stared at his own watch. Since a lunar day and night together fill twenty-eight Earth days of time, a strictly lunar "day" contains nearly three hundred forty Earth-hours. To call one-twelfth of that period an hour would be an affectation. To call each twenty-four Earth hours a day would have been absurd. So the actual period of the moon's rotation was divided into familiar time-intervals, and a bulletin-board in the hotel lobby in Lunar City notified those interested that: *Sunday will be from 143 o'clock to 167 o'clock A.M.* There would be another Sunday some time during the lunar afternoon.

Cochrane debated momentarily whether this information could be used in the publicity campaign of Spaceways, Inc. Strictly speaking, there was some slight obligation to throw extra fame Dabney's way regardless, because the corporation had been formed as a public-relations device. Any other features, such as changing the history of the human race, were technically incidental. But Cochrane put his watch away. To talk about horology on the moon wouldn't add to Dabney's stature as a phoney scientist. It didn't matter.

He went back to the business at hand. Some two years before there had been a fake corporation organized strictly for the benefit of its promoters. It had built a rocket-ship ostensibly for the establishment of a colony on Mars. The ship had managed to stagger up to Luna, but no farther. Its promoters had sold stock on the promise that a ship that could barely reach Luna could take off from that small glove with six times as much fuel as it could lift off of Earth. Which was true. Investors put in their money on that verifiable fact. But the truth happened to be, of course, that it would still take an impossible amount of fuel to accelerate the ship—so heavily loaded—to a speed where it would reach Mars in one human lifetime. Taking off from Luna would solve only the problem of gravity. It wouldn't do a thing about inertia. So the ship never rose from its landing near Lunar City. The corporation that had built it went profitably bankrupt.

Cochrane had been working feverishly to find out who owned that ship now. Just before the torp-test he'd mentioned, he found that the ship belonged to the hotel desk-clerk, who had bought it in hopes of renting it sooner or later for television background-shots in case anybody was crazy enough to make a television film-tape on the moon. He was now discouraged. Cochrane chartered it, putting up a bond to return it undamaged. If the ship was lost, the hotel-clerk would get back his investment—about a week's pay.

So Cochrane had a space-ship practically in his pocket when the public demonstration of the Dabney field came off at half-past 203 o'clock.

The site of the demonstration was the shadowed, pitch-dark part of the floor of a crater twenty miles across, with walls some ten thousand jagged feet high. The furnace-like sunshine made the plain beyond the shadow into a sea of blinding brightness. The sunlit parts of the crater's walls were no less terribly glaring. But above the edge of the cliffs the stars began; infinitely small and many-colored, with innumerable degrees of brightness. The Earth hung in mid-sky like a swollen green apple, monstrous in size. And the figures which moved about the scene of the test could be seen only faintly by reflected light from the lava plain, because one's eyes had to be adjusted to the white-hot moon-dust on the plain and mountains.

There were not many persons present. Three jeeps waited in the semi-darkness, out of the burning sunshine. There were no more than a dozen moon-suited individuals to watch and perform the test of the Dabney field. Cochrane had scrupulously edited all fore-news of the experiment to give Dabney the credit he had paid for. There were present, then, the party from Earth—Cochrane and Babs and Holden, with the two tame scientists and Bell

45

the writer—and the only two reporters on the moon. Only news syndicates could stand the expense-account of a field man in Lunar City. And then there were Jones and Dabney and two other figures apparently brought by Dabney.

There was, of course, no sound at all on the moon itself. There was no air to carry it. But from each plastic helmet a six-inch antenna projected straight upward, and the microwaves of suit-talkies made a jumble of slightly metallic sounds in the headphones of each suit.

As soon as Cochrane got out of the jeep's airlock and was recognized, Dabney said agitatedly:

"Mr. Cochrane! Mr. Cochrane! I have to discuss something with you! It is of the utmost importance! Will you come into the laboratory?"

Cochrane helped Babs to the ground and made his way to the airlock in the dust-heap against the cliff. He went in, with two other space-suited figures who detached themselves from the rest to follow him. Once inside the odorous cramped laboratory, Dabney opened his face-plate and began to speak before Cochrane was ready to hear him. His companion beamed amiably.

"—and therefore, Mr. Cochrane," Dabney was saying agitatedly, "I insist that measures be taken to protect my scientific reputation! If this test should fail, it will militate against the acceptance of my discovery! I warn you—and I have my friend Mr. Simms here as witness—that I will not be responsible for the operation of apparatus made by a subordinate who does not fully comprehend the theory of my discovery! I will not be involved—"

Cochrane nodded. Dabney, of course, didn't understand the theory of the field he'd bought fame-rights to. But there was no point in bringing that up. Johnny Simms beamed at both of them. He was the swimmer Babs had pointed out in the swimming-pool. His face was completely unlined and placid, like the face of a college undergraduate. He had never worried about anything. He'd never had a care in the world. He merely listened with placid interest.

"I take it," said Cochrane, "that you don't mind the test being made, so long as you don't have to accept responsibility for its failure—and so long as you get the credit for its success if it works. That's right, isn't it?"

"If it fails, I am not responsible!" insisted Dabney stridently. "If it succeeds, it will be because of my discovery."

Cochrane sighed a little. This was a shabby business,

but Dabney would have convinced himself, by now, that he was the genius he wanted people to believe him.

"Before the test," said Cochrane gently, "you make a speech. It will be recorded. You disclaim the crass and vulgar mechanical details and emphasize that you are like Einstein, dealing in theoretic physics only. That you are naturally interested in attempts to use your discovery, but your presence is a sign of your interest but not your responsibility."

"I shall have to think it over——," began Dabney nervously.

"You can say," promised Cochrane, "that if it does not work you will check over what Jones did and tell him why."

"Y-yes," said Dabney hesitantly, "I could do that. But I must think it over first. You will have to delay——"

"If I were you," said Cochrane confidentially, "I would plan a speech to that effect because the test is coming off in five minutes."

He closed his face-plate as Dabney began to protest. He went into the lock. He knew better than to hold anything up while waiting for a neurotic to make a decision. Dabney had all he wanted, now. From this moment on he would be frantic for fear of losing it. But there could be no argument outside the laboratory. In the airlessness, anything anybody said by walkie-talkie could be heard by everybody.

When Dabney and Simms followed out of the lock, Cochrane was helping Jones set up the device that had been prepared for this test. It was really two devices. One was a very flat cone, much like a coolie-hat and hardly larger, with a sort of power-pack of coils and batteries attached. The other was a space-ship's distress-signal rocket, designed to make a twenty-mile streak of red flame in emptiness. Nobody had yet figured out what good a distress signal would do, between Earth and moon, but the idea was soothing. The rocket was four feet long and six inches in diameter. At its nose there was a second coolie-hat cone, with other coils and batteries.

Jones set the separate cone on the ground and packed stones around and under it to brace it. His movements were almost ridiculously deliberate. Bending over, he bent slowly, or the motion would lift his feet off the ground. Straightening up, he straightened slowly, or the upward impetus of his trunk would again lift him beyond contact with solidity. But he braced the flat cone carefully.

He set the signal-torpedo over that cone. The entire set-up was under six feet tall, and the coolie-hat cones were no more than eighteen inches in diameter. He said flatly:

"I'm all ready."

The hand and arm of a space-suited figure lifted, for attention. Dabney's voice came worriedly from the headphones of every suit:

"I wish it understood," he said in some agitation, "that this first attempted application of my discovery is made with my consent, but that I am not aware of the mechanical details. As a scientist, my work has been in pure science. I have worked for the advancement of human knowledge, but the technological applications of my discovery are not mine. Still—if this device does not work, I will take time from my more important researches to inquire into what part of my discovery has been inadequately understood and applied. It may be that present technology is not qualified to apply my discovery——"

Jones said without emotion—but Cochrane could imagine his poker-faced expression inside his helmet:

"That's right. I consulted Mr. Dabney about the principles, but the apparatus is my doing. I take the responsibility for that!"

Then Cochrane added with pleasant irony:

"Since all this is recorded, Mr. Dabney can enlarge upon his disinterest later. Right now, we can go ahead. Mr. Dabney disavows us unless we are successful. Let us let it go at that." Then he said: "The observatory's set to track?"

A muffled voice said boredly, by short-wave from the observatory up on the crater's rim:

"We're ready. Visual and records, and we've got the timers set to clock the auto-beacon signals as they come in."

The voice was not enthusiastic. Cochrane had had to put up his own money to have the nearside lunar observatory put a low-power telescope to watch the rocket's flight. In theory, this distress-rocket should make a twenty-mile streak of relatively long-burning red sparks. A tiny auto-beacon in its nose was set to send microwave signals at ten-second intervals. On the face of it, it had looked like a rather futile performance.

"Let's go," said Cochrane.

He noted with surprise that his mouth was suddenly

48

dry. This affair was out of all reason. A producer of television shows should not be the person to discover in an abstruse scientific development the way to reach the stars. A neurotic son-in-law of an advertising tycoon should not be the instrument by which the discovery should come about. A psychiatrist should not be the means of associating Jones—a very junior physicist with no money—and Cochrane and the things Cochrane was prepared to bring about if only this unlikely-looking gadget worked.

"Jones," said Cochrane with a little difficulty, "let's follow an ancient tradition. Let Babs christen the enterprise by throwing the switch."

Jones pointed there in the shadow of the crater-wall, and Babs moved to the switch he indicated. She said absorbedly:

"Five, four, three, two, one—"

She threw the switch. There was a spout of lurid red flame.

The rocket vanished.

It vanished. It did not rise, visibly. It simply went away from where it was, with all the abruptness of a light going out. There was a flurry of the most brilliant imaginable carmine flame. That light remained. But the rocket did not so much rise as disappear.

Cochrane jerked his head up. He was close to the line of the rocket's ascent. He could see a trail of red sparks which stretched to invisibility. It was an extraordinarily thin line. The separate flecks of crimson light which comprised it were distant in space. They were so far from each other that the signal-rocket was a complete failure as a device making a streak of light that should be visible.

The muffled voice in the helmet-phones said blankly:

"Hey! What'd you do to that rocket?"

The others did not move. They seemed stunned. The vanishing of the rocket was no way for a rocket to act. In all expectation, it should have soared skyward with a reasonable velocity, and should have accelerated rather more swiftly from the moon's surface than it would have done from Earth. But it should have remained visible during all its flight. Its trail should have been a thick red line. Instead, the red sparks were so far separated—the trail was so attenuated—that it was visible only from a spot near its base. The observatory voice said more blankly still:

"Hey! I've picked up the trail! I can't see it nearby, but it seems to start, thin, about fifty miles up and go on

away from there! That rocket shouldn't ha' gone more than twenty miles! What happened?"

"*Watch for the microwave signals,*" said Jones' voice in Cochrane's headphones.

The voice from the observatory squeaked suddenly. This was not one of the highly-placed astronomers, but part of the mechanical staff who'd been willing to do an unreasonable chore for pay.

"Here's the blip! It's crazy! Nothing can go that fast!"

And then in the phones there came the relayed signal of the auto-beacon in the vanished rocket. The signal-sound was that of a radar pulse, beginning at low pitch and rising three octaves in the tenth of a second. At middle C—the middle of the range of a piano—there was a momentary spurt of extra volume. But in the relayed signal that louder instant had dropped four tones. Cochrane said crisply:

"Jones, what speed would that be?"

"*It'd take a slide-rule to figure it,*" said Jones' voice, very calmly, "*but it's faster than anything ever went before.*"

Cochrane waited for the next beep. It did not come in ten seconds. It was easily fifteen. Even he could figure out what that meant! A signal-source that stretched ten seconds of interval at source to fifteen at reception . . .

The voice from the observatory wailed:

"It's crazy! It can't be going like that!"

They waited. Fifteen seconds more. Sixteen. Eighteen. Twenty. The beep sounded. The spurt of sound had dropped a full octave. The signal-rocket, traveling normally, might have attained a maximum velocity of some two thousand feet per second. It was now moving at a speed which was an appreciably large fraction of the speed of light. Which was starkly impossible. It simply happened to be true.

They heard the signal once more. The observatory's multiple-receptor receiver had been stepped up to maximum amplification. The signal was distinct, but very faint indeed. And the rocket was then traveling—so it was later computed—at seven-eighths of the speed of light. Between the flat cone on the front of the distress-torpedo, and the flat cone on the ground, a field of force existed. The field was not on the back surface of the torpedo's cone, but before the front surface. It went back to the moon from there, so all the torpedo and its batteries were in the columnar stressed space. And an amount of rocket-push that should have sent the four-foot torpedo maybe twenty miles during

50

its period of burning, had actually extended its flight to more than thirty-seven hundred miles before the red sparks were too far separated to be traced any farther, and by then had kicked the torpedo up impossibly close to light-speed.

In a sense, the Dabney field had an effect similar to the invention of railways. The same horsepower moved vastly more weight faster, over steel rails, than it could haul over a rutted dirt road. The same rocket-thrust moved more weight faster in the Dabney field than in normal space. There would be a practical limit to the speed at which a wagon could be drawn over a rough road. The speed of light was a limit to the speed of matter in normal space. But on a railway the practical speed at which a vehicle could travel went up from three miles an hour to a hundred and twenty. In the Dabney field it was yet to be discovered what the limiting velocity might be. But old formulas for acceleration and increase-of-mass-with-velocity simply did not apply in a Dabney field.

Jones rode back to Lunar City with Cochrane and Holden and Babs. His face was dead-pan.

Babs tried to recover the mien and manner of the perfect secretary.

"Mr. Cochrane," she said professionally, "will you want to read the publicity releases Mr. Bell turns out from what Mr. West and Mr. Jamison tell him?"

"I don't think it matters," said Cochrane. "The newsmen will pump West and Jamison empty, anyhow. It's all right. In fact, it's better than our own releases would be. They'll contradict each other. It'll sound more authentic that way. We're building up a customer-demand for information."

The small moon-jeep rolled and bumped gently down the long, improbable highway back to Lunar City. Its engine ran smoothly, as steam-engines always do. It ran on seventy per cent hydrogen peroxide, first developed as a fuel back in the 1940s for the pumps of the V2 rockets that tried to win the Second World War for Germany. When hydrogen peroxide comes in contact with a catalyst, such as permanganate of potash, it breaks down into oxygen and water. But the water is in the form of high-pressure steam, which is used in engines. The jeep's fuel supplied steam for power and its ashes were water to drink and oxygen to breathe. Steam ran all motorized vehicles on Luna.

"What are you thinking about, Jones?" asked Cochrane suddenly.

Jones said meditatively:

"I'm wondering what sort of field-strength a capacity-storage system would give me. I boosted the field intensity this time. The results were pretty good. I'm thinking—suppose I made the field with a strobe-light power-pack—or maybe a spot-welding unit. Even a portable strobe-light gives a couple of million watts for the forty-thousandth of a second. Suppose I fixed up a storage-pack to give me a field with a few billion watts in it? It might be practically like matter-transmission, though it would really be only high-speed travel. I think I've got to work on that idea a little . . ."

Cochrane digested the information in silence.

"Far be it from me," he said presently, "to discourage such high-level contemplation. Bill, what's on your mind?"

Holden said moodily:

"I'm convinced that the thing works. But Jed! You talk as if you hadn't any more worries! Yet even if you and Jones do have a way to make a ship travel faster than light, you haven't got a ship or the capital you need—."

"I've got scenery that looks like a ship," said Cochrane mildly. "Consider that part settled."

"But there are supplies. Air—water—food—a crew—. We can't pay for such things! Here on the moon the cost of everything is preposterous! How can you try out this idea without more capital than you can possibly raise?"

"I'm going to imitate my old friend Christopher Columbus," said Cochrane. "I'm going to give the customers what they want. Columbus didn't try to sell anybody shares in new continents. Who wanted new continents? Who wanted to move to a new world? Who wants new planets now? Everybody would like to see their neighbors move away and leave more room, but nobody wants to move himself. Columbus sold a promise of something that had an already-established value, that could be sold in every town and village—that had a merchandising system already set up! I'm going to offer just such a marketable commodity. I'll have freight-rockets on the way up here within twenty-four hours, and the freight and their contents will all be paid for!"

He turned to Babs. He looked more sardonic and cynical than ever before.

"Babs, you've just witnessed one of the moments that

52

ought to be illustrated in all the grammar-school history-books along with Ben Franklin flying a kite. What's top-most in your mind?"

She hesitated and then flushed. The moon-jeep crunched and clanked loudly over the trail that led downhill. There was no sound outside, of course. There was no air. But the noise inside the moon-vehicle was notable. The steam-motor, in particular, made a highly individual racket.

"I'd—rather not say," said Babs awkwardly. "What's your own main feeling, Mr. Cochrane?"

"Mine?" Cochrane grinned. "I'm thinking what a hell of a funny world this is, when people like Dabney and Bill and Jones and I are the ones who have to begin operation outer space!"

CHAPTER FOUR

COCHRANE SAID KINDLY INTO THE VISION-BEAM MICRO-phone to Earth, "Cancel section C, paragraph nine. Then section b(1) from paragraph eleven. Then after you've canceled the entire last section—fourteen—we can sign up the deal."

There was a four-second pause. About two seconds for his voice to reach Earth. About two seconds for the beginning of the reply to reach him. The man at the other end protested wildly.

"We're a long way apart," said Cochrane blandly, "and our talk only travels at the speed of light. You're not talking from one continent to another. Save tolls. Yes or no?"

Another four-second pause. The man on Earth profanely agreed. Cochrane signed the contract before him. The other man signed. Not only the documents but all conversation was recorded. There were plugged-in witnesses. The contract was binding.

Cochrane leaned back in his chair. His eyes blinked wearily. He'd spent hours going over the facsimile-transmitted contract with Joint Networks, and had weeded out a total of six joker-stipulations. He was very tired. He yawned.

"You can tell Jones, Babs," he said, "that all the high financing's done. He can spend money. And you can transmit my resignation to Kursten, Kasten, Hopkins and Fallowe. And since this is a pretty risky operation, you'd better send a service message asking what you're to do with yourself. They'll probably tell you to take the next rocket back and report to the secretarial pool, I'm afraid. The same fate probably awaits West and Jamison and Bell."

Babs said guiltily:

"Mr. Cochrane—you've been so busy I had to use my own judgment. I didn't want to interrupt you—."

"What now?" demanded Cochrane.

"The publicity on the torp-test," said Babs guiltily, "was so good that the firm was worried for fear we'd seem to be doing it for a client of the firm—which we are. So we've all been put on a leave-with-expenses-and-pay status. Officially, we're all sick and the firm is paying our expenses until we regain our health."

"Kind of them," said Cochrane. "What's the bite?"

"They're sending up talent contracts for us to sign," admitted Babs. "When we go back, we would command top prices for interviews. The firm, of course, will want to control that."

Cochrane raised his eyebrows.

"I see! But we'll actually be kept off the air so Dabney can be television's fair-haired boy. He'll go on Marilyn Winter's show, I'll bet, because that has the biggest audience on the planet. He'll lecture Little Aphrodite Herself on the constants of space and she'll flutter her eyelashes at him and shove her chest-measurements in his direction and breathe how wonderful it is to be a man of science!"

"How'd you know?" demanded Babs, surprised.

Cochrane winced.

"Heaven help me, Babs, I didn't. I tried to guess at something too impossible even for the advertising business! But I failed! I failed! You and my official gang, then, are here with the firm's blessing, free of all commands and obligations, but drawing salary and expenses?"

"Yes," admitted Babs. "And so are you."

"I get off!" said Cochrane firmly. "Forward my resignation. It's a matter of pure vanity. But Kursten, Kasten, Hopkins and Fallowe do move in a mysterious way to latch onto a fast buck! I'm going to get some sleep. Is there anything else you've had to use your judgment on?"

"The contracts for re-broadcast of the torp-test. The original broadcast had an audience-rating of seventy-one!"

"Such," said Cochrane, "are the uses of fame. Our cash?"

She showed him a neatly typed statement. For the original run of the torp-test film-tape, so much. It was to be re-run with a popularization of the technical details by West, and a lurid extrapolation of things to come by Jamison. The sponsors who got hold of commercial time with that expanded and souped-up version would expect, and get, an audience-rating unparalleled in history. Dabney was to take a bow on the rebroadcast, too—very much the dignified and aloof scientist. There were other interviews.

Dabney again, from a script written by Bell. And Jones. Jones hated the idea of being interviewed, but he had faced a beam-camera and answered idiotic questions, and gone angrily back to his work.

Spaceways, Inc., had a bank-account already amounting to more than twenty years of Cochrane's best earning-power. He was selling publicity for sponsors to hang their commercials on, in a strict parallel to Christopher Columbus', selling of spices to come. But Cochrane was delivering for cash. Freight-rockets were on the way moonward now, whose cargoes of supplies for a space-journey Cochrane was accepting only when a bonus in money was paid for the right to brag about it. So-and-so's oxygen paid for the privilege of supplying air-reserves. What's-his-name's dehydrated vegetables were accepted on similar terms, with whoosit's instant coffee and somebody else's noodle soup in bags.

"If," said Cochrane tiredly, looking up from the statement, "we could only start off in a fleet instead of a single ship, Babs, we'd not only be equipped but so rich before we started that we'd want to stay home to enjoy it!" He yawned prodigiously. "I'm going to get some sleep. Don't let me sleep too long!"

He went off to his hotel-room and was out cold before his head had drifted down to its pillow. But he was not pleased with himself. It annoyed him that his revolt against being an expendable employee had taken the form of acting like one of his former bosses in collecting ruthlessly for the brains—in the case of Jones—and the neurotic idiosyncrasies—in the case of Dabney—of other men. The gesture by which he had become independent was not quite the splendid, scornful one he'd have liked. The fact that this sort of gesture worked, and nothing else would have, did not make him feel better.

But he slept.

He dreamed that he was back at his normal business of producing a television show. Nobody but himself cared whether the show went on or not. The actual purpose of all his subordinates seemed to be to cut as many throats among their fellow-workers as possible—in a business way, of course—so that by their own survival they might succeed to a better job and higher pay. This is what is called the fine spirit of teamwork by which things get done, both in private and public enterprise.

It was a very realistic dream, but it was not restful.

While he slept, the world wagged on and the cosmos continued on its normal course. The two moons of Earth—one natural and one artificial—swung in splendid circles. The red spot of Jupiter and the bands on that gas-giant world moved in orderly fashion about its circumference. Light-centuries away, giant Cepheid suns expanded monstrously and contracted again, rather more rapidly than their gravitational fields could account for. Double stars sedately swung about each other. Comets reached their farthest points and, mere aggregations of frigid jagged stones and metal, prepared for another plunge back into light and heat and warmth.

And various prosaic actions took place on Luna.

When Cochrane waked and went back to the hotel-room in use as an office, he found Babs talking confidentially to a woman—girl, rather—whom Cochrane vaguely remembered. Then he did a double take. He did remember her. Three or four years before she'd been the outstanding television personality of the year. She'd been pretty, but not so pretty that you didn't realize that she was a person. She was everything that Marilyn Winters was not—and she'd been number two name in television.

Cochrane said blankly:

"Aren't you Alicia Keith?"

The girl smiled faintly. She wasn't as pretty as she had been. She looked patient. And an expression of patience, on a woman's face, is certainly not unpleasant. But it isn't glamorous, either.

"I was," she said. "I married Johnny Simms."

Cochrane looked at Babs.

"They live up here," explained Babs. "I pointed him out at the swimming-pool the day we got here."

"Wonderful," said Cochrane. "How——"

"Johnny," said Alicia, "has bought into your Spaceways corporation. He got your man West drunk and bought his shares of Spaceway stock."

Cochrane sat down—not hard, because it was impossible to sit down hard on the moon. But he sat down as hard as it was possible to sit.

"Why'd he do that?"

"He found out you had hold of the old Mars colony ship. He understands you're going to take a trip out to the stars. He wants to go along. He's very much like a little boy. He hates it here."

"Then why live——." Cochrane checked the question, not quite in time.

"He can't go back to Earth," said Alicia calmly. "He's a psychopathic personality. He's sane and quite bright and rather dear in his way, but he simply can't remember what is right and wrong. Especially when he gets excited. When they fixed up Lunar City as an international colony, by sheer oversight they forgot to arrange for extradition from it. So Johnny can live here. He can't live anywhere else—not for long."

Cochrane said nothing.

"He wants to go with you," said Alicia pleasantly. "He's thrilled. The lawyer his family keeps up here to watch over him is thrilled, too. He wants to go back and visit his family. And as a stockholder, Johnny can keep you from taking a ship of any other corporate property out of the jurisdiction of the courts. But he'd rather go with you. Of course I have to go too."

"It's blackmail," said Cochrane without heat. "A pretty neat job of it, too. Babs, you see Holden about this. He's a psychiatrist." He turned to Alicia. "Why do you want to go? I don't know whether it'll be dangerous or not."

"I married Johnny," said Alicia. Her smile was composed. "I thought it would be wonderful to be able to trust somebody that nobody else could trust." After a moment she added: "It would be, if one could."

A few moments later she went away, very pleasantly and very calmly. Her husband had no sense of right or wrong—not in action, anyhow. She tried to keep him from doing too much damage by exercising the knowledge she had of what was fair and what was not. Cochrane grimaced and told Babs to make a note to talk to Holden. But there were other matters on hand, too. There were waivers to be signed by everybody who went along off Luna. Then Cochrane said thoughtfully:

"Alicia Keith would be a good name for film-tape . . ."

He plunged into the mess of paper-work and haggling which somebody has to do before any achievement of consequence can come about. Pioneer efforts, in particular, require the same sort of clearing-away process as the settling of a frontier farm. Instead of trees to be chopped and dug up by the roots, there are the gratuitous obstructionists who have to be chopped off at the ankles in a business way, and the people who exercise infinite ingenuity trying to get a

58

cut of something—anything—somebody else is doing. And of course there are the publicity-hounds. Since Spaceways was being financed on sales of publicity which could be turned on this product and that, publicity-hounds cut into its revenue and capital.

Back on Earth a crackpot inventor had a lawyer busily garnering free advertisement by press conferences about the injury done his client by Spaceways, Inc., who had stolen his invention to travel through space faster than light. Somebody in the Senate made a speech accusing the Spaceway project of being a political move by the party in power for some dire ultimate purpose.

Ultimately the crackpot inventor would get on the air and announce triumphantly that only part of his invention had been stolen, because he'd been too smart to write it down or tell anybody, and he wouldn't tell anybody—not even a court—the full details of his invention unless paid twenty-five million in cash down, and royalties afterward. The project for a congressional investigation of Spaceways would die in committee.

But there were other griefs. The useless space-ship hulk had to be emptied of the mining-tools stored in it. This was done by men working in space-suits. Occupational rules required them to exert not more than one-fourth of the effort they would have done if working for themselves. When the ship was empty, air was released in it, and immediately froze to air-snow. So radiant heaters had to be installed and powered to warm up the hull to where an atmosphere could exist in it. Its generators had to be thawed from the metal-ice stage of brittleness and warmed to where they could be run without breaking themselves to bits.

But there were good breaks, too. Presently a former moonship-pilot—grounded to an administrative job on Luna—on his own free time checked over the ship. Jones arranged it. With rocket-motors of adamite—the stuff discovered by pure accident in a steel-mill back on Earth—the propelling apparatus checked out. The fuel-pumps had been taken over in fullness of design from fire-engine pumps on Earth. They were all right. The air-regenerating apparatus had been developed from the aerating culture-tanks in which antibiotics were grown on Earth. It needed only reseeding with algae—microscopic plants which when supplied with ultraviolet light fed avidly on carbon dioxide

59

and yielded oxygen. The ship was a rather involved combination of essentially simple devices. It could be put back into such workability as it had once possessed with practically no trouble.

It was.

Jones moved into it, with masses of apparatus from the laboratory in the Lunar Apennines. He labored lovingly, fanatically. Like most spectacular discoveries, the Dabney field was basically simple. It was almost idiotically uncomplicated. In theory it was a condition of the space just outside one surface of a sheet of metal. It was like that conduction-layer on the wires of a cross-country power-cable, when electricity is transmitted in the form of high-frequency alterations and travels on the skins of many strands of metal, because high-frequency current simply does not flow inside of wires, but only on their surfaces. The Dabney field formed on the surface—or infinitesimally beyond it —of a metal sheet in which eddy-currents were induced in such-and-such a varying fashion. That was all there was to it.

So Jones made the exterior forward surface of the abandoned spaceship into a generator of the Dabney field. It was not only simple, it was too simple! Having made the bow of the ship into a Dabney field plate, he immediately arranged that he could, at will, make the rear of the ship into another Dabney field plate. The two plates, turned on together, amounted to something that could be contemplated with startled awe, but Jones planned to start off, at least, in a manner exactly like the distress-torp test. The job of wiring up for faster-than-light travel, however, was not much more difficult than wiring a bungalow, when one knew how it should be done.

Two freight-rockets came in, picked up by radar and guided to landings by remote control. The Lunar City beam receiver picked up music aimed up from Earth and duly relayed it to the dust-heaps which were the buildings of the city. The colonists and moon-tourists became familiar with forty-two new tunes dealing with prospective travel to the stars. One work of genius tied in a just-released film-tape drama titled *"Child of Hate"* to the Lunar operation, and charmed listeners saw and heard the latest youthful tenor gently plead, *"Child of Hate, Come to the Stars and Love."* The publicity department responsible for the masterpiece considered itself not far from genius, too.

There was confusion thrice and four and five times confounded. Cochrane came in to dispute furiously with Holden whether it was better to have a psychopathic personality on the space-ship or to have a legal battle in the courts. Cochrane won. Jones arrived, belligerent, to do battle for technical devices which would cost money.

"Look!" said Cochrane harassedly. "I'm not trying to boss you! Don't come to me for authority! If you can make that ship take off I'll be in it, and my neck will be in as much danger as yours. You buy what will keep my neck as safe as possible, along with yours. I'm busy raising money and fighting off crackpots and dodging lawsuits and getting supplies! I've got a job that needs three men anyhow. All I'm hoping is that you get ready to take off before I start cutting out paperdolls. When can we leave?"

"We?" said Jones suspiciously. "You're going?"

"If you think I'll stay behind and face what'll happen if this business flops," Cochrane told him, "you're crazy! There are too many people on Earth already. There's no room for a man who tried something big and failed! If this flops I'd rather be a frozen corpse with a happy smile on my face—I understand that in space one freezes—than somebody living on assisted survival status on Earth!"

"Oh," said Jones, mollified. "How many people are to go?"

"Ask Bill Holden," Cochrane told him. "Remember, if you need something, get it. I'll try to pay for it. If we come back with picture-tapes of outer space—even if we only circumnavigate Mars!—we'll have money enough to pay for anything!"

Jones regarded Cochrane with something almost like warmth.

"I like this way of doing business," he said.

"It's not business!" protested Cochrane. "This is getting something done! By the way, have you picked out a destination for us to aim at?" When Jones shook his head, Cochrane said harassedly, "Better get one picked out. But when we make out our sail-off papers, for destination we'll say, 'To the stars.' A nice line for the news broadcasts. Oh, yes. Tell Bill Holden to try to find us a skipper. An astrogator. Somebody who can tell us how to get back if we get anywhere we need to get back from. Is there such a person?"

"I've got him," said Jones. "He checked the ship for

61

me. Former moon-rocket pilot. He's here in Lunar City. Thanks!"

He shook hands with Cochrane before he left. Which for Jones was an expression of overwhelming emotion. Cochrane turned back to his desk.

"Let's see . . . That arrangement for cachets on stamps and covers to be taken along and postmarked Outer Space. Put in a stipulation for extra payment in case we touch on planets and invent postmarks for them . . ."

He worked on, while Babs took notes. Presently he was dictating. And as he talked, frowning, he took a fountain-pen from his pocket and absently worked the refill-handle. It made ink exude from the pen-point. On the moon, the surface tension of the ink was exactly the same as on earth, but the gravity was five-sixths less. So a drop of ink of really impressive size could be formed before the moon's weak gravity made it fall.

Dictating as he worked the pen, Cochrane achieved a pear-shaped mass of ink which was quite the size of a large grape before it fell into his waste-basket. It was the largest he'd made to date. It fell—slow-motion—and splashed—violently—as he regarded it with harried satisfaction.

More time passed. A moon-rocket arrived from Earth. There were new tourists under the thousand-foot plastic dome. Out by the former Mars-ship Jones made experiments with small plastic balloons coated with a conducting varnish. In a vacuum, a cubic inch of air at Earth-pressure will expand to make many cubic feet of near-vacuum. If a balloon can sustain an internal pressure of one ounce to the square foot, a thimbleful of air will inflate a sizeable globe to that pressure. Jones was arranging tiny Dabney field robot-generators with tiny atomic batteries to power them. Each such balloon would be a Dabney field "plate" when cast adrift in emptiness, and its little battery would keep it in operation for twenty years or more.

Baggage came up from Earth for Johnny Simms. It was mostly elephant-guns and ammunition for them. Johnny, as the heir to innumerable millions back on earth, had had a happy life, but hardly one to give him a practical view of things. To him, star-travel meant landing on such exotic planets as the fictioneers had been writing about for a hundred years or so. He really looked upon the venture into space as a combined big-game expedition and escape from Lunar City. And he did look forward, too, to freedom from his family's legal representative and the constant reminder of ethical and moral values which Johnny preferred happily to ignore.

Film-tape came up, and cameras to use it in. Every imaginable item an expedition to space could use or even might use, was thrust upon Spaceways, Inc. Manufacturers yearned to have their products used in connection with the hottest news story in decades. There was a steady trailing of moon-jeeps from the airlocks of Lunar City to the ship.

The time of lunar sunset arrived—503:30 o'clock, half-past five hundred and three hours. Time was measured from midnight to midnight, astronomical fashion. The great, blazing sun whose streamer prominences, even, were too bright to be looked at with the naked eye—the sun neared and reached the horizon. There was no change in the star-studded sky. There were no sunset colorings. The incandescent brightness on the mountains was not lessened in the least. Only the direction of the stark black shadows shifted.

The glaring sun descended. Its motion was almost infinitely slow. Its disk was of the order of half a degree of arc, and it took a full hour to be fully obscured. And then there was at first no difference in the look of things save that the *Mare Imbrium*—the solidified, arid Sea of Showers —was as dark as the shadows in the mountains.

They still gleamed brightly. For a very long time the white-hot sunshine glowed on their flanks. The brightness rose and rose, and blackness followed it. At long last only the topmost peaks of the Apennines blazed luridly against a background of stars whose light seemed feeble by comparison.

Then it was night indeed. But the Earth shone forth, a half-globe of seas and clouds and continents, vast and nostalgic in the sky. And now Earthshine fell upon the moon. It was many times brighter than moonlight ever was upon the Earth. Even at lunar sunset the Earthlight was sixteen times brighter. At midnight, when the Earth was full, it would be bright enough for any activity. Actually, the human beings on Luna were nearly nocturnal in their habits, because it was easier to run moon-jeeps in frigidity and keep men and machines warm enough for functioning, than it was to protect them against the more-than-boiling heat of midday on the moon.

So the activity about the salvaged space-ship increased. There were electric lights blazing in the demi-twilight, to guide freight vehicles with their loads. The tourist-jeeps went and returned and went and returned. The last shipload of travelers from Earth wanted to see the space-craft about which all the world was talking.

Even Cochrane presently became curious. There came a time when all the paper-work connected with what had happened was done with, and conditional contracts drawn up on everything that could be foreseen. It was time for something new to happen.

Cochrane said dubiously:

"Babs, have you seen the ship?"

She shook her head.

"I think we'd better go take a look at it," said Cochrane. "Do you know, I've been acting like a damned business man! I've only been out of Lunar City three times. Once to the laboratory to talk, once to test a signal-rocket across the crater, and once when the distress-torp went off. I haven't even seen the nightclub here in the City!"

"You should," said Babs matter-of-factly. "I went once, with Doctor Holden. The dancing was marvelous!"

"Bill Holden, eh?" said Cochrane. He found himself annoyed. "Took you to the nightclub, but not to see the ship!"

"The ship's farther," explained Babs. "I could always be found at the nightclub if you needed me. I went when you were asleep."

"Damn!" said Cochrane. "Hm . . . You ought to get a bonus. What would you rather have, Babs, a bonus in cash or Spaceways stock?"

"I've got some stock," said Babs. "Mr. Bell—the writer, you know—got in a poker game. He was cleaned out. So I gave him all the money I had—I told you I cleared out my savings-account before we came up, I think—for half his shares."

"Either you got very badly stuck," Cochrane told her cynically, "or else you'll be so rich you won't speak to me."

"Oh, no!" said Babs warmly. "Never!"

Cochrane yawned.

"Let's get out and take a look at the ship. Maybe I can stow cargo or something, now there's no more paper-work."

Babs said with an odd calm:

"Mr. Jones wanted you out there today—in an hour, he said. I promised you'd go. I meant to mention it in time."

Cochrane did not notice her tone. He was dead-tired, as only a man can be who has driven himself at top speed for days on end over a business deal. Business deals are stimulating only in their major aspects. Most of the details are niggling, tedious, routine, and boring—and very often bear-trapped. Cochrane had done, with only Babs' help, an amount of mental labor that in the offices of Kursten, Kasten, Hopkins and Fallowe would have been divided among two vice-presidents, six lawyers, and at least twelve account executives. The work, therefore, would actually have been done by not less than twenty secretaries. But Babs and Cochrane had done it all.

In the moon-jeep on the way to the ship he felt that heavy, exhausted sense of relaxation which is not pleasurable at all. Babs annoyed him a little, too. She was late getting to the airlock, and seemed breathless when she arrived.

The moon-jeep crunched and clanked and rumbled over the gently undulating lava sea beneath its giant wheels. Babs looked zestfully out of the windows. The picture was, of course, quite incredible. In the relatively dim Earthlight the moonscape was somehow softened, and yet the impossibly jagged mountains and steep cliffsides and the razor-edged passes of monstrous stone,—these things remained daunting. It was like riding through a dream in which everything nearby seemed fey and glamorous, but the background was deathly-still and ominous.

There were the usual noises inside the jeep. The air had a metallic smell. One could detect the odors of oil, and ozone, and varnish, and plastic upholstery. There were the crunching sounds of the wheels, traveling over stone. There was the paradoxic gentleness of all the jeep's motions because of the low gravity. Cochrane even noted the extraordinary feel of an upholstered seat when one weighs only one-sixth as much as back on Earth. All his sensations were dreamlike—but he felt that headachy exhaustion that comes of overwork too long continued.

"I'll try," he said tiredly, "to see that you have some fun before you go back, Babs. You'll go back as soon as we dive off into whatever we're diving into, but you ought to get in the regular tourist stuff up here, anyhow."

Babs said nothing. Pointedly.

The moon-jeep clanked and rumbled onward. The hissing of steam was audible. The vehicle swung around a pinnacle of stone, and Cochrane saw the space-ship.

In the pale Earthlight it was singularly beautiful. It had been designed to lure investors in a now-defunct promotion. It was stream-lined, and gigantic, and it glittered like silver. It stood upright on its tail-fins, and it had lighted ports and electric lights burned in the emptiness about it. But there was only one moon-jeep at its base. A space-suited figure moved toward a dangling sling and sat in it. He rose deliberately toward an open airlock-hatch, and the other moon-jeep moved soundlessly away back toward Lunar City.

There was no debris about. There was no cargo waiting to be loaded. Cochrane did see a great metal plate, tilted on the ground, with a large box attached to it by cables. That would be the generators and the field-plate for a Dabney field. It was plainly to remain on the moon. It was not underneath the ship. Cochrane puzzled tiredly over it for a moment. Then he understood. The ship would lift on its rockets, hover over the plate—which would be generating its half of the field—and then Jones would switch on the apparatus in the ship itself. The forward, needle-pointed nose of the ship would become another generator of the Dabney field. The ship's inertia, in that field, would be effectively reduced to a fraction of its former value. The rockets, which might give it an acceleration of a few hundred feet per second anywhere but in a Dabney field, would immediately accelerate the ship and all its contents to an otherwise unattainable velocity. The occupants of the rocket would lose their relative inertia to the same degree as the ship. They should feel no more acceleration than from the same rocket-thrust in normal space. But they would travel—

Cochrane felt that there was a fallacy, somehow, in the working of the Dabney field as he understood it. If there was less enertia in the Dabney field—why—a rocket shouldn't push as hard in it because it was the inertia of the rocket-gases that gave the rocket-thrust. But Cochrane was much too tired to work out a theoretic objection to something he knew did work. He was almost dozing when Babs touched his arm.

"Space-suits, Mr. Cochrane."

He got wearily into the clumsy costume. But he saw again that Babs wore the shining-eyed look of rapturous adventure that he had seen her wear before.

They got out of the moon-jeep, one after the other.

The sling came down the space-ship's gleaming side. They got in it, together. It lifted them.

The vast, polished hull of the space-ship slid past them only ten feet away. The ground diminished. They seemed less to be lifted than to float skyward. And in this sling, in this completely unreal ascent, Cochrane roused suddenly. He felt the acute unease which comes of height. He had looked down upon Earth from a height of four thousand miles with no feeling of dizziness. He had looked at Earth a quarter-million miles away with no consciousness of depth. But a mere fifty feet above the surface of the moon he felt like somebody swinging out of a skyscraper window.

Then the airlock opening was beside them, and the sling rolled inward. They were in the lock, and Cochrane found himself pushing Babs away from the unrailed opening. He was relieved when the airlock closed.

Inside the ship, with the space-suits off, there was light and warmth, and a remarkably matter-of-fact atmosphere. The ship had been built to sell stock in a scheme for colonizing Mars. Prospective investors had been shown through it. It had been designed to be a convincing passenger-liner of space.

It was. But Cochrane found himself not needed for any consultation, and Jones was busy, and Bill Holden highly preoccupied. He saw Alicia Keith—but her name was Simms now. She smiled at him but took Babs by the arm. They went off somewhere.

Cochrane waited for somebody to tell him what to look at and to admire. He saw Jamison, and Bell, and he saw a man he had not seen before. He settled down in a deeply upholstered chair. He felt neglected. Everybody was busy. But mostly he felt tired.

He slept.

Then Babs was shaking his arm, her eyes shining.

"Mr. Cochrane!" she cried urgently. "Mr. Cochrane! Wake up! Go on up to the control-room! We're going to take off!"

He blinked at her.

"We!" Then he started up, and went five feet into the air from the violence of his uncalculated movement. "We? No you don't! You go back to Lunar City where you'll be safe!"

Then he heard a peculiar drumming, rumbling noise. He had heard it before. In the moonship. It was rockets being tested; being burned; rockets in the very last seconds of preparation before take-off for the stars.

He didn't drop back to the floor beside the chair he'd occupied. The floor rose to meet him.

"I've had our baggage brought on board," said Babs, happily. "I'm going because I'm a stockholder! Hold on to something and climb those stairs if you want to see us go up! I'm going to be busy!"

CHAPTER FIVE

THE PHYSICAL SENSATIONS OF ASCENDING TO THE SHIP'S
control-room were weird in the extreme. Cochrane had just
been wakened from a worn-out sleep, and it was always
startling on the moon to wake and find one's self weighing
one-sixth of normal. It took seconds to remember how
one got that way. But on the way up the stairs, Cochrane
was further confused by the fact that the ship was surging
this way and swaying that. It moved above the moon's
surface to get over the tilted flat Dabney field plate on the
ground a hundred yards from the ship's original position.

The Dabney field, obviously, was not in being. The
ship hovered on its rockets. They had been designed to
lift it off the Earth—and they had—against six times the
effective gravity here, and with an acceleration of more
gravities on top of that. So the ship rose lightly, almost
skittishly. When gyros turned to make it drift sidewise—
as a helicopter tilts in Earth's atmosphere—it fairly
swooped to a new position. Somebody jockeyed it this way
and that.

Cochrane got to the control-room by holding on with
both hands to railings. He was angry and appalled.

The control-room was a hemisphere, with vertical vision-
screens picturing the stars overhead. Jones stood in an odd
sort of harness beside a set of control-switches that did not
match the other smoothly designed controls of the ship. He
looked out of a plastic blister, by which he could see around
and below the ship. He made urgent signals to a man
Cochrane had never seen before, who sat in a strap-chair
before many other complex controls with his hands playing
back and forth upon them. A loudspeaker blatted unmusi-
cally. It was Dabney's voice, highly agitated and uneasy.

"... *my work for the advancement of science has been
applied by other minds. I need to specify that if the experiment now about to begin does not succeed, it will not in-*

validate my discovery, which has been amply verified by other means. It may be, indeed, that my discovery is so far ahead of present engineering——."

"See here!" raged Cochrane. "You can't take off with Babs on board! This is dangerous!"

Nobody paid any attention. Jones made frantic gestures to indicate the most delicate of adjustments. The man in the strap-chair obeyed the instructions with an absorbed attention. Jones suddenly threw a switch. Something lighted, somewhere. There was a momentary throbbing sound which was not quite a sound.

"Take it away," said Jones in a flat voice.

The man in the strap-chair pressed hard on the controls. Cochrane glanced desperately out of one of the side ports. He saw the moonscape—the frozen lava sea with its layer of whitish-tan moondust. He saw many moon-jeeps gathered near, as if most of the population of Lunar City had been gathered to watch this event. He saw the extraordinary nearness of the moon's horizon.

But it was the most momentary of glimpses. As he opened his mouth to roar a protest, he felt the upward, curiously comforting thrust of acceleration to one full Earth-gravity.

The moonscape was snatched away from beneath the ship. It did not descend. The ship did not seem to rise. The moon itself diminished and vanished like a pricked bubble. The speed of its disappearance was not—it specifically was not—attributable to one Earth-gravity of lift applied on a one-sixth-gravity moon.

The loudspeaker hiccoughed and was silent. Cochrane uttered the roar he had started before the added acceleration began. But it was useless. Out the side-port, he saw the stars. They were not still and changeless and winking, as they appeared from the moon. These stars seemed to stir uneasily, to shift ever so slightly among themselves, like flecks of bright color drifting on a breeze.

Jones said in an interested voice:

"Now we'll try the booster."

He threw another switch. And again there was a momentary throbbing sound which was not quite a sound. It was actually a sensation, which one seemed to feel all through one's body. It lasted only the fraction of a second, but while it lasted the stars out the side-ports ceased to be stars. They became little lines of light, all moving toward the ship's stern but at varying rates of speed. Some of them

70

passed beyond view. Some of them moved only a little. But all shifted.

Then they were again tiny spots of light, of innumerable tints and colors, of every conceivable degree of brightness, stirring and moving ever-so-slightly with relation to each other.

"The devil!" said Cochrane, raging.

Jones turned to him. And Jones was not quite poker-faced, now. Not quite. He looked even pleased. Then his face went back to impassiveness again.

"It worked," he said mildly.

"I know it worked!" sputtered Cochrane. "But—where are we? How far did we come?"

"I haven't the least idea," said Jones mildly as before. "Does it matter?"

Cochrane glared at him. Then he realized how completely too late it was to protest anything.

The man he had seen absorbed in the handling of controls now lifted his hands from the board. The rockets died. There was a vast silence, and weightlessness. Cochrane weighed nothing. This was free flight again—like practically all of the ninety-odd hours from the space platform to the moon. The pilot left the controls and in an accustomed fashion soared to a port on the opposite side of the room. He gazed out, and then behind, and said in a tone of astonished satisfaction:

"This is good!—There's the sun!"

"How far?" asked Jones.

"It's fifth magnitude," said the pilot happily. "We really did pile on the horses!"

Jones looked momentarily pleased again. Cochrane said in a voice that even to himself sounded outraged:

"You mean the sun's a fifth-magnitude star from here? What the devil happened?"

"Booster," said Jones, nearly with enthusiasm. "When the field was just a radiation speed-up, I used forty milliamperes of current to the square centimetre of field-plate. That was the field-strength when we sent the signal-rocket across the crater. For the distress-torpedo test, I stepped the field-strength up. I used a tenth of an ampere per square centimetre. I told you! And don't you remember that I wondered what would happen if I used a capacity-storage system?"

Cochrane held fast to a hand-hold.

"The more power you put into your infernal field," he demanded, "the more speed you get?"

Jones said contentedly:

"There's a limit. It depends on the temperature of the things in the field. But I've fixed up the field, now, like a spot-welding outfit. Like a strobe-light. We took off with a light field. It's on now—we have to keep it on. But I got hold of some pretty storage condensers. I hooked them up in parallel to get a momentary surge of high-amperage current when I shorted them through my field-making coils. Couldn't make it a steady current! Everything would blow! But I had a surge of probably six amps per square centimetre for a while."

Cochrane swallowed.

"The field was sixty times as strong as the one the distress-torpedo used? We went—we're going—sixty times as fast?"

"We had lots more speed than that!" But then Jones' enthusiasm dwindled. "I haven't had time to check," he said unhappily. "It's one of the things I want to get at right away. But in theory the field should modify the effect of inertia as the fourth power of its strength. Sixty to the fourth is—."

"How far," demanded Cochrane, "is Proxima Centauri? That's the nearest star to Earth. How near did we come to reaching it?"

The pilot on the other side of the control-room said with a trace less than his former zest:

"That looks like Sirius, over there . . ."

"We didn't head for Proxima Centauri," said Jones mildly. "It's too close! And we have to keep the field-plate back on the moon lined up with us, more or less, so we headed out roughly along the moon's axis. Toward where its north pole points."

"Then where are we headed? Where are we going?"

"We're not going anywhere just yet," said Jones without interest. "We have to find out where we are, and from that—"

Cochrane ran his hand through his hair.

"Look!" he protested. "Who's running this show? You didn't tell me you were going to take off! You didn't pick out a destination! You didn't—"

Jones said very patiently:

"We have to try out the ship. We have to find out how fast it goes with how much field and how much rocket-

72

thrust. We have to find out how far we went and if it was in a straight line. We even have to find out how to land! The ship's a new piece of apparatus. We can't do things with it until we find out what it can do."

Cochrane stared at him. Then he swallowed.

"I see," he said. "The financial and business department of Spaceways, Inc., has done its stuff for the time being."

Jones nodded.

"The technical staff now takes over?"

Jones nodded again.

"I still think," said Cochrane, "that we could have done with a little interdepartmental cooperation. How long before you know what you're about?"

Jones shook his head.

"I can't even guess. Ask Babs to come up here, will you?"

Cochrane threw up his hands. He went toward the spiral-ladder-with-handholds that led below. He went down into the main saloon. A tiny green light winked on and off, urgently, on the far side. Babs was seated at a tiny board, there. As Cochrane looked, she pushed buttons with professional skill. Bill Holden sat in a strap-chair with his face a greenish hue.

"We took off," said Holden in a strained voice.

"We did," said Cochrane. "And the sun's a fifth magnitude star from where we've got to—which is no place in particular. And I've just found out that we started off at random and Jones and the pilot he picked up are now happily about to do some pure-science research!"

Holden closed his eyes.

"When you want to cheer me up," he said feebly, "you can tell me we're about to crash somewhere and this misery will soon be over."

Cochrane said bitterly:

"Taking off without a destination! Letting Babs come along! They don't know how far we've come and they don't know where we're going! This is a hell of a way to run a business!"

"Who called it a business?" asked Holden, as feebly as before. "It started out as a psychiatric treatment!"

Babs' voice came from the side of the saloon where she sat at a vision-tube and microphone. She was saying professionally:

"I assure you it's true. We are linked to you by the

Dabney field, in which radiation travels much faster than light. When you were a little boy didn't you ever put a string between two tin cans, and then talk along the string?"

Cochrane stopped beside her, scowling. She looked up.

"The press association men on Luna, Mr. Cochrane. They saw us take off, and the radar verified that we traveled some hundreds of thousands of miles, but then we simply vanished! They don't understand how they can talk to us without even the time-lag between Earth and Lunar City. I was explaining."

"I'll take it," said Cochrane. "Jones wants you in the control-room. Cameras? Who was handling the cameras?"

"Mr. Bell," said Babs briskly. "It's his hobby, along with poker-playing and children."

"Tell him to get some pictures of the star-fields around us," said Cochrane, "and then you can see what Jones wants. I will do a little business!"

He settled down in the seat Babs had vacated. He faced the two press-association reporters in the screen. They had seen the ship's takeoff. It was verified beyond any reasonable question. The microwave beam to Earth was working at capacity to transmit statements from the Moon Observatory, which annoyedly conceded that the Spaceways, Inc., salvaged ship had taken off with an acceleration beyond belief. But, the astronomers said firmly, the ship and all its contents must necessarily have been destroyed by the shock of their departure. The acceleration must have been as great as the shock of a meteor hitting Luna.

"You can consider," Cochrane told them, "that I am now an angel, if you like. But how about getting a statement from Dabney?"

A press-association man, back on Luna, uttered the first profanity ever to travel faster than light.

"All he can talk about," he said savagely, "is how wonderful he is! He agrees with the Observatory that you must all be dead. He said so. Can you give us any evidence that you're alive and out in space? Visual evidence, for broadcast?"

At this moment the entire fabric of the space-ship moved slightly. There was no sound of rockets. The ship seemed to turn a little, but that was all. No gravity. No acceleration. It was a singularly uncomfortable sensation, on top of the discomfort of weightlessness.

Cochrane said sardonically:

"If you can't take my word that I'm alive, I'll try to get you some proof! Hm. I'll send you some pictures of the star-fields around us. Shoot them to observatories back on Earth and let them figure out for themselves where we are! Displacement of the relative positions of the stars ought to let them figure things out!"

He left the communicator-board. Holden still looked greenish in his strap-chair. The main saloon was otherwise empty. Cochrane made his way gingerly to the stair going below. He stepped into thin air and descended by a pull on the hand-rail.

This was the dining-saloon. The ship having been built to impress investors in a stock-sales enterprise, it had been beautifully equipped with trimmings. And, having had to rise from Earth to Luna, and needing to take an acceleration of a good many gravities, it had necessarily to be reasonably well-built. It had had, in fact, to be an honest job of ship-building in order to put across a phoney promotion. But there were trimmings that could have been spared. The ports opening upon emptiness, for example, were not really practical arrangements. But everybody but Holden and the two men in the control-room now clustered at those ports, looking out at the stars. There was Jamison and Bell the writer, and Johnny Simms and his wife. Babs had been here and gone.

Bell was busy with a camera. As Cochrane moved to tell him of the need for star-shots to prove to a waiting planet that they were alive, Johnny Simms turned and saw Cochrane. His expression was amiable and unawed.

"Hello," said Johnny Simms cheerfully.

Cochrane nodded curtly.

"I bought West's stock in Spaceways," said Johnny Simms, amusedly, "because I want to come along. Right?"

"So I heard," said Cochrane, as curtly as before.

"West said," Johnny Simms told him gleefully, "that he was going back to Earth, punch Kursten, Kasten, Hopkins and Fallowe on their separate noses, and then go down to South Carolina and raise edible snails for the rest of his life."

"An understandable ambition," said Cochrane. He frowned, waiting to talk to Bell, who was taking an infernally long time to focus a camera out of a side-port.

"It's going to be good when he tries to cash my check," said Johnny Simms delightedly. "I stopped payment on it

75

when he wouldn't pick up the tab for some drinks I invited him to have!"

Cochrane forced his face to impassiveness. Johnny Simms was that way, he understood. He was a psychopathic personality. He was completely insensitive to notions of ethics. Ideas of right and wrong were as completely meaningless to him as tones to a tone-deaf person, or pastel tints to a man who is color-blind. They simply didn't register. His mind was up to par, and he could be a charming companion. He could experience the most kindly of emotions and most generous of impulses, which he put into practice. But he also had a normal person's impulse to less admirable behavior, and he simply could not understand that there was any difference between impulses. He put the unpleasing ones into practice too. He'd been on the moon to avoid extradition because of past impulses which society called murderous. On this ship it was yet to be discovered what he would do—but because he was technically sane his lawyers could have prevented a takeoff unless he came along. Cochrane, at the moment, felt an impulse to heave him out an airlock as a probable danger. But Cochrane was not a psychopathic personality.

He stopped Bell in his picture-taking and looked at the first of the prints. They were excellent. He went back to the vision-set to transmit them back to Luna. He sent them off. They would be forwarded to observatories on Earth and inspected. They literally could not be faked. There were thousands of stars on each print—with the Milky Way for background on some—and each of those thousands of stars would be identified, and each would have changed its relative position from that seen on earth, with relation to every other star. Astronomers could detect the spot from which the picture had been taken. But to fake a single print would have required years of computation and almost certainly there would have been slipups somewhere. These pictures were unassailable evidence that a human expedition had reached a point in space that had been beyond all human dreaming.

Then Cochrane had nothing to do. He was a supernumerary member of the crew. The pilot and Jones were in charge of the ship. Jamison would take care of the catering, when meal-time came. Probably Alicia Keith—no, Alicia Simms—would help. Nothing else needed attention. The rockets either worked or they didn't. The air-apparatus

76

needed no supervision. Cochrane found himself without a function.

He went restlessly back to the control-room. He found Babs looking helpless, and Jones staring blankly at a slip of paper in his hands, while the pilot was still at a blister-port, staring at the stars through one of those squat, thick telescopes used on Luna for the examination of the planets.

"How goes the research?" asked Cochrane.

"We're stumped," said Jones painfully. "I forgot something."

"What?"

"Whenever I wanted anything," said Jones, "I wrote it out and gave a memo to Babs. She attended to it."

"My system, exactly," admitted Cochrane.

"I wrote out a memo for her," said Jones unhappily, "asking for star-charts and for her to get somebody to set up a system of astrogation for outside the solar system. Nobody's ever bothered to do that before. Nobody's ever reached even Mars! But I figured we'd need it."

Cochrane waited. Jones showed him a creased bit of paper, closely written.

"I wrote out the memo and put it in my pocket," said Jones, "and I forgot to give it to Babs. So we can't astro-gate. We don't know how. We didn't get either star-charts or instructions. We're lost."

Cochrane waited.

"Apparently Al was mistaken in the star he spotted as our sun," added Jones. He referred to the pilot, whom Cochrane had not met before. "Anyhow we can't find it again. We turned the ship to look at some more stars, and we can't pick it out any more."

Cochrane said:

"You'll keep looking, of course."

"For what?" asked Jones.

He waved his hand out the four equally-spaced plastic blister-ports. From where he stood, Cochrane could see thousands of thousands of stars out those four small openings. They were of every conceivable color and degree of brightness. The Milky Way was like a band of diamonds.

"We know the sun's a yellow star," said Jones, "but we don't know how bright it should be, or what the sky should look like beyond it."

"Constellations?" asked Cochrane.

"Find 'em!" said Jones vexedly.

Cochrane didn't try. If a moonrocket pilot could not

spot familiar star-groups, a television producer wasn't likely to see them. And it was obvious, once one thought, that the brighter stars seen from Earth would be mostly the nearer ones. If Jones was right in his guess that his booster had increased the speed of the ship by sixty to the fourth power, it would have gone some millions of times as fast as the distress-torpedo, for a brief period (the ratio was actually something over nineteen million times) and it happened that nobody had been able to measure the speed of that test-object.

Cochrane was no mathematician, but he could see that there was no data for computation on hand. After one found out how fast an acceleration of one Earth-gravity in a Dabney field of such-and-such strength speeded up a ship, something like dead reckoning could be managed. But all that could be known right now was that they had come a long way.

He remembered a television show he'd produced, laid in space on an imaginary voyage. The script-writer had had one of the characters say that no constellation would be visible at a hundred light-years from the solar system. It would be rather like a canary trying to locate the window he'd escaped from, from a block away, with no memories of the flight from it.

Cochrane said suddenly, in a pleased tone:

"This is a pretty good break—if we can keep them from finding out about it back home! We'll have an entirely new program, good for a thirteen-week sequence, on just this!"

Babs stared at him.

"Main set, this control-room," said Cochrane enthusiastically. "We'll get a long-beard scientist back home with a panel of experts. We'll discuss our problems here! We'll navigate from home, with the whole business on the air! We'll have audience-identification up to a record! Everybody on Earth will feel like he's here with us, sharing our problems!"

Jones said irritably:

"You don't get it! We're lost! We can't check our speed without knowing where we are and how far we've come! We can't find out what the ship will do when we can't find out what it's done! Don't you see?"

Cochrane said patiently:

"I know! But we're in touch with Luna through the Dabney field that got us here! It transmitted radiation before, faster than light. It's transmitting voice and pictures now. Now we set up a television show which pays for our astrogation and lets the world sit in on the prettier aspects of our travels. Hm . . . How long before you can sit down on a planet, after you have all the navigational aids of— say—the four best observatories on Earth to help you? I'll arrange for a sponsor—."

He went happily down the stairs again. This was a spiral stair, and he zestfully spun around it as he went to the next deck below. At the bottom he called up to Babs:

"Babs! Get Bell and Alicia Keith and come along to take dictation! I'm going to need some legal witnesses for the biggest deal in the history of advertising, made at several times the speed of light!"

And he went zestfully to the communicator to set it up.

And time passed. Data arrived, which at once solved Jones' and the pilot's problem of where they were and how far they had come—it was, actually, 178.3 light-years— and they spent an hour making further tests and getting further determinations, and then they got a destination.

They stopped in space to extrude from the airlock a small package which expanded into a forty-foot plastic balloon with a minute atomic battery attached to it. The plastic was an electric conductor. It was a field-plate of the Dabney field. It took over the field from Earth and maintained it. It provided a second field for the ship to maintain. The ship, then, could move at any angle from the balloon. The Dabney field stretched 178.3 light-years through emptiness to the balloon, and then at any desired direction to the ship.

The ship's rockets thrust again—and the booster-circuit came into play. There were maneuverings. A second balloon was put out in space.

At 8:30 Central U. S. Time, on a period relinquished by other advertisers—bought out—a new program went on the air. It was a half-hour show, sponsored by the Intercity Credit Corporation—"Buy on Credit Guaranteed" —with ten straight minutes of commercials interjected in four sections. It was the highest-priced show ever put on the air. It showed the interior of the ship's control-room, with occasional brief switches to authoritative persons on Earth for comment on what was relayed from the far-off skies.

The first broadcast ensured the success of the program beyond possible dispute. It started with curt conversation between Jones and the pilot, Al—Jones loathed this part of it, but Al turned out to be something of a ham—on the problems of approaching a new solar system. Cut to computers back on Earth. Back to the control-room of the star-ship. Pictures of the local sun, and comments on its differentness from the sun that had nourished the human race since time began.

Then the cameras—Bell worked them—panned down through the ship's blister-ports. There was a planet below. The ship descended toward it. It swelled visibly as the space-ship approached. Cochrane stood out of camera-range and acted as director as well as producer of the opus. He used even Johnny Simms as an offstage voice repeating stern commands. It was corny. There was no doubt about it. It had a large content of ham.

But it happened to be authentic. The ship had reached another planet, with vast ice-caps and what appeared to be no more than a twenty-degree-wide equatorial belt where there was less than complete glaciation. The rockets roared and boomed as the ship let down into the cloud-layers.

Television audiences back on Earth viewed the new planet nearly as soon as did those in the ship. The time-lag was roughly three seconds for a distance of 203.7 light-years.

The surface of the planet was wild and dramatic beyond belief. There were valleys where vegetation grew luxuriantly. There were ranges of snow-clad mountains interpenetrating the equatorial strip, and there were masses of white which, as the ship descended, could be identified as glaciers moving down toward the vegetation.

But as the ship sank lower and lower—and the sound of its rockets became thunderous because of the atmosphere around it—a new feature took over the central position in one's concept of what the planet was actually like.

The planet was volcanic. There were smoking cones everywhere—in the snow-fields, among the ice-caps, in between the glaciers, and even among the tumbled areas whose greenness proved that here was an environment which might be perilous, but where life should thrive abundantly.

The ship continued to descend toward a great forest near a terminal moraine.

CHAPTER SIX

JAMISON DECLAIMED, WEARING A THROAT-MIKE AS BELL zestfully panned his camera and the ship swung down. It was an impressive broadcast. The rockets roared. With the coming of air about the ship, they no longer made a mere rumbling. They created a tumult which was like the growl of thunder if one were in the midst of the thunder-cloud. It was a numbing noise. It was almost a paralyzing noise. But Jamison talked with professional smoothness.

"This planet," he orated, while pictures from Bell's camera went direct to the transmitter below, "this planet is the first world other than Earth on which a human ship has landed. It is paradoxic that before men have walked on Mars' red iron-oxide plains and breathed its thin cold air, or fought for life in the formaldehyde gales of Venus, that they should look upon a world which welcomes them from illimitable remoteness. Here we descend, and all mankind can watch our descent upon a world whose vegetation is green; whose glaciers prove that there is air and water in plenty, whose very smoking volcanoes assure us of its close kinship to Earth!"

He lifted the mike away from his throat and framed words with his lips. *"Am I still on?"* Cochrane nodded. Cochrane wore headphones carrying what the communicator carried, as this broadcast went through an angled Dabney field relay system back to Lunar City and then to Earth. He spoke close to Jamison's ear.

"Go ahead! If your voice fades, it will be the best possible sign-off. Suspense. Good television!"

Jamison let the throat-mike back against his skin. The roaring of the rockets would affect it only as his throat vibrated from the sound. It would register, even so.

"I see," said Jamison above the rocket-thunder, "forests of giant trees like the sequoias of Mother Earth. I see rushing rivers, foaming along their rocky beds, taking their rise in glaciers. We are still too high to look for living creatures, but we descend swiftly. Now we are level with the highest of the mountains. Now we descend below their smoking tops. Under us there is a vast valley, miles wide, leagues long. Here a city could be built. Over it looms a gigantic mountain-spur, capped with green. One would expect a castle to be built there."

He raised his eyebrows at Cochrane. They were well in atmosphere, now, and it had been an obvious defect— condition—necessity of the Dabney field that both of its plates should be in a vacuum. One was certainly in air now. But Cochrane made that gesture which in television production-practice informs the actors that time to cutting is measured in tens of seconds, and he held up two fingers. Twenty seconds.

"We gaze, and you gaze with us," said Jamison, "upon a world that future generations will come to know as home —the site of the first human colony among the stars!"

Cochrane began to beat time. Ten, nine, eight—.

"We are about to land," Jamison declaimed. "We do not know what we shall find—What's that?" He paused dramatically. "A living creature?—A living creature sighted down below! We sign off now—from the stars!"

The ending had been perfectly timed. Allowing for a three-second interval for the broadcast to reach the moon, and just about two more for it to be relayed to Earth, his final word, "Stars!" had been uttered at the precise instant to allow a four-minute commercial by Intercity Credit, in the United States, by Citroen in Europe, by Fabricanos Unidos in South and Central America, and Near East Oil along the Mediterranean. At the end of that four minutes it would be time for station identification and a time-signal, and the divers eight-second flashes before other programs came on the air.

The rockets roared and thundered. The ship went down and down. Jamison said:

"I thought we'd be cut off when we hit air!"

"That's what Jones thought," Cochrane assured him. He bellowed above the outside tumult, "Bell! See anything alive down below?"

Bell shook his head. He stayed at the camera aimed out a blister-port, storing up film-tape for later use. There was the feel of gravitation, now. Actually, it was the fact that the ship slowed swiftly in its descent.

Cochrane went to a port. The ship continued its descent.

"Living creature? Where?"

Jamison shrugged. He had used it as a sign-off line. An extrapolation from the fact that there was vegetation below. He looked somehow distastefully out the port at a swiftly rising green ground below. He was a city man. He had literally never before seen what looked like habitable territory of such vast extent, with no houses on it. In a valley easily ten miles long and two wide, there was not a square inch of concrete or of glass. There was not a man-made object in view. The sky was blue and there were clouds, but to Jamison the sight of vegetation implied rooftops. There ought to be parapets where roofs ended to let light down to windows and streets below. He had never before seen grass save on elevated recreation-areas, nor bushes not arranged as landscaping, and certainly not trees other than the domesticated growths which can grow on the tops of buildings. To Jamison this was desolation. On the moon, absence of structures was understandable. There was no air. But here there should be a city!

The ship swayed a little as the rockets swung their blasts to balance the descending mass. The intended Mars-ship slowed, and slowed, and hovered—and there was terrifying smoke and flame suddenly all about—and then there was a distinct crunching impact. The rockets continued to burn, their ferocity diminished. They slackened again. And yet again. They were reduced to a mere faint murmur.

There was a remarkable immobility of everything. It was the result of gravity. Earth-value gravity, or very near it. There was a distinct pressure of one's feet against the floor, and a feeling of heaviness to one's body which was very different from Lunar City, and more different still from free flight in emptiness.

Nothing but swirling masses of smoke could be seen out the ports. They had landed in a forest, of sorts, and the rocket-blasts had burned away everything underneath, down to solid soil. In a circle forty yards about the ship the ground was a mass of smoking, steaming ash. Beyond that flames licked hungrily, creating more dense vapor. Beyond that still there was only coiling smoke.

Cochrane's headphones yielded Babs' voice, almost wailing:

"Mr. Cochrane! We must have landed! I want to see!"

Cochrane pressed the hand-mike button.

"Are we still hooked up to Lunar City?" he demanded. "We can't be, but are we?"

"We are," said Babs' voice mutinously. *"The broadcast went through all right. They want to talk to you. Everybody wants to talk to you!"*

"Tell them to call back later," commanded Cochrane. "Then leave the beam working—however it works!—and come up if you like. Tell the moon operator you'll be away for ten minutes."

He continued to stare out the window. Al, the pilot, stayed in his cushioned seat before the bank of rocket-controls. The rockets were barely alight. The ship stayed as it had landed, upright on its triple fins. He said to Jones:

"It feels like we're solid. We won't topple!"

Jones nodded. The rocket-sound cut off. Nothing happened.

"I think we could have saved fuel on that landing," said Jones. Then he added, pleased, "Nice! The Dabney field's still on! It has to be started in a vacuum, but it looks like it can hold air away from itself once it's established. Nice!"

Babs rushed up the stairs. She gazed impassionedly out of a vision-port. Then she said disappointedly:

"It looks like—"

"It looks like hell," said Cochrane. "Just smoke and steam and stuff. We can hope, though, that we haven't started a forest fire, but have just burned off a landing-place."

They stared out. Presently they went to another port and gazed out of that. The smoke was annoying, and yet it could have been foreseen. A moon-rocket, landing at its space-port on Earth, heated the tarmac to red-hotness in the process of landing. Tender-vehicles had to wait for it to cool before they could approach. Here the ship had landed in woodland. Naturally its flames had seared the spot where it came down. And there was inflammable stuff about, which caught fire. So the ship was in the situation of a phoenix, necessarily nesting in a conflagration. Anywhere it landed the same thing would apply, unless it tried landing on a glacier. But then it would settle down into a lake of boiling water, amid steam, and could expect to be frozen in as soon as its landing-place cooled.

Now there was nothing to do. They had to wait. Once the whole ship quivered very slightly, as if the ground trembled faintly under it. But there was nothing at which to be alarmed.

84

They could see that this particular forest was composed mainly of two kinds of trees which burned differently. One had a central trunk, and it burned with resinous flames and much black and gray-black smoke. The other was a curious growth—a solid, massive trunk which did not touch ground at all, but was held up by aerial roots which supported it aloft through very many slender shafts widely spread. Possibly the heavier part was formed on the ground and lifted as its air-roots grew.

It was irritating, though, to be unable to see from the ship so long as the fire burned outside. The pall of smoke lasted for a long time. In three hours there were no longer any fiercely blazing areas, but the ashes still smouldered and smoke still rose. In three hours and a half, the local sun began to set. There were colorings in the sky, beyond all comparison glorious. Which was logical enough. When Krakatoa, back on Earth, blew itself to bits in the eighteen hundreds, it sent such volumes of dust into the air that sunsets all around the globe were notably improved for three years afterward. On this planet, smoking cones were everywhere visible. Volcanic dust, then, made nightfall magnificent past description. There was not only gold and crimson in the west. The zenith itself glowed carmine and yellow, and those in the space-ship gazed up at a sky such as none of them could have imagined possible.

The colors changed and changed, from yellow to gold all over the sky, and still the glory continued. Presently there was a deep, deep red, deep past imagining, and presently faint bluish stars pierced it, and they stared up at new strange constellations—some very bright indeed—and all about the ship there was a bed of white ash with glowing embers in it, and a thin sheet of white smoke still flowed away down the valley.

It was long after sunset when Cochrane got up from the communicator. Communication with Earth was broken at last. There was a balloon out in space somewhere with an atomic battery maintaining all its surface as a Dabney field plate. The ship maintained a field between itself and that plate. The balloon maintained another field between itself and another balloon a mere 178.3 light-years from the solar system. But the substance of this planet intervened between the nearer balloon and the ship. Jones made tests and observed that the field continued to exist, but was plugged by the matter of this newly-arrived-at world.

Come tomorrow, when there was no solid-stone barrier to the passage of radiation, they could communicate with Earth again.

But Cochrane was weary and now discouraged. So long as talk with Earth was possible, he'd kept at it. There was a great deal of talking to be done. But a good deal of it was extremely unsatisfactory.

He found Bill Holden having supper with Babs, on the floor below the communicator. Very much of the recent talk had been over Cochrane's head. He felt humiliated by the indignation of scientists who would not tell him what he wanted to know without previous information he could not give.

When he went over to the dining-table, he felt that he creaked from weariness and dejection. Babs looked at him solicitously, and then jumped up to get him something to eat. Everybody else was again watching out the ship's ports at the new, strange world of which they could see next to nothing.

"Bill," said Cochrane fretfully, "I've just been given the dressing-down of my life! You're expecting to get out of the airlock in the morning and take a walk. But I've been talking to Earth. I've been given the devil for landing on a strange planet without bringing along a bacteriologist, an organic chemist, an ecologist, an epidemiologist, and a complete laboratory to test everything with, before daring to take a breath of outside air. I'm warned not to open a port!"

Holden said:

"You sound as if you'd been talking to a biologist with a reputation. You ought to know better than that!"

Cochrane protested:

"I wanted to talk to somebody who knew more than I did! What could I do but get a man with a reputation?"

Holden shook his head.

"We psychiatrists," he observed, "go around peeping under the corners of rugs at what people try to hide from themselves. We have a worm's-eye view of humanity. We know better than to throw a difficult problem at a man with an established name! They're neurotic about their reputations. Like Dabney, they get panicky at the idea of anybody catching them in a mistake. No big name in medicine or biology would dare tell you that of course it's all right for us to take a walk in the rather pretty landscape outside."

"Then who will?" demanded Cochrane.

"We'll make what tests we can," said Holden comfortingly, "and decide for ourselves. We can take a chance. We're only risking our lives!"

Babs brought Cochrane a plate. He put food in his mouth and chewed and swallowed.

"They say we can't afford to breathe the local air at all until we know its bacteriology; we can't touch anything until we test it as a possible allergen; we can't."

Holden grunted.

"What would those same authorities have told your friend Columbus? On a strange continent he'd be sure to find strange plants and strange animals. He'd find strange races of men and he ought to find strange diseases. They'd have warned him not to risk it. *They* wouldn't!"

Cochrane ate with a sort of angry vigor. Then he snapped:

"If you want to know, we've got to land! We're sunk if we don't go outside and move around! We'll spoil our story-line. This is the greatest adventure-serial anybody on Earth ever tuned in to follow! If we back down on exploration, our audience will be disgusted and resentful and they'll take it out on our sponsors!"

Babs said softly, to Holden:

"That's my boss!"

Cochrane glared at her. He didn't know how to take the comment. He said to Holden:

"Tomorrow we'll try to figure out some sort of test and try the air. I'll go out in a space-suit and crack the face-plate! I can close it again before anything lethal gets in. But there's no use stepping out into a bed of coals tonight. I'll have to wait till morning."

Holden smiled at him. Babs regarded him with intent, enigmatic eyes.

Neither of them said anything more. Cochrane finished his meal. Then he found himself without an occupation. Gravity on this planet was very nearly the same as on Earth. It felt like more, of course, because all of them had been subject only to moon-gravity for nearly three weeks. Jones and the pilot had been in one-sixth gravity for a much longer time. And the absence of gravity had caused their muscles to lose tone by just about the amount that the same time spent in a hospital bed would have done. They felt physically worn out.

It was a healthy tiredness, though, and their muscles

87

would come back to normal as quickly as one recovers strength after illness—rather faster, in fact. But tonight there would be no night-life on the space-ship. Johnny Simms disappeared, after symptoms of fretfulness akin to those of an over-tired small boy. Jamison gave up, and Bell, and Al the pilot fell asleep while Jones was trying to discuss something technical with him. Jones himself yawned and yawned and when Al snored in his face he gave up. They retired to their bunks.

There was no point in standing guard over the ship. If the bed of hot ashes did not guard it, it was not likely that an individual merely sitting up and staring out its ports would do much good. There were extremely minor, practically unnoticeable vibrations of the ship from time to time. They would be volcanic temblors—to be expected. They were not alarming, certainly, and the forest outside was guarantee of no great violence to be anticipated. The trees stood firm and tall. There was no worry about the ship. It was perfectly practical, and even necessary simply to turn out the lights and go to sleep.

But Cochrane could not relax. He was annoyed by the soreness of his muscles. He was irritated by the picture given him of the expedition as a group of heedless igno-ramuses who'd taken off without star-charts or bacterio-logical equipment—without even apparatus to test the air of planets they might land on!—and who now were sternly warned not to make any use of their achievement. Cochrane was not overwhelmed by the achievement itself, though less than eighteen hours before the ship and all its company had been aground on Luna, and now they were landed on a new world twice as far from Earth as the Pole Star.

It is probable that Cochrane was not awed because he had a television-producer's point of view. He regarded this entire affair as a production. He was absorbed in the de-tails of putting it across. He looked at it from his own, quite narrow, professional viewpoint. It did not disturb him that he was surrounded by a wilderness. He considered the wilderness the set on which his production belonged, though he was as much a city man as anybody else. He went back to the control-room. With the ship standing on its tail that was the highest point, and as the embers burned out and the smoke lessened it was possible to look out into the night.

He stared at the dimly-seen trees beyond the burned

area, and at the dark masses of mountains which blotted out the stars. He estimated them, without quite realizing it, in view of what they would look like on a television screen. When light objects in the control-room rattled slightly, he paid no attention. His rehearsal-studio had been rickety, back home.

Babs seemed to be sleepless, too. There was next to no light where Cochrane was—merely the monitor-lights which assured that the Dabney field still existed, though blocked for use by the substance of a planet. Babs arrived in the almost-dark room only minutes after Cochrane. He was moving restlessly from one port to another, staring out.

"I thought I'd tell you," Babs volunteered, "that Doctor Holden put some algae from the air-purifier tanks in the airlock, and then opened the outer door."

"Why?" asked Cochrane.

"Algae's Earth plant-life," explained Babs. "If the air is poisonous, it will be killed by morning. We can close the outer door of the lock, pump out the air that came from this planet, and then let air in from the ship so we can see what happens."

"Oh," said Cochrane.

"And then I couldn't sleep," said Babs guilelessly. "Do you mind if I stay here? Everybody else has gone to bed."

"Oh, no," said Cochrane. "Stay if you like."

He stared out at the dark. Presently he moved to another port. After a moment he pointed.

"There's a glow in the sky there," he said curtly.

She looked. There was a vast curving blackness which masked the stars. Beyond it there was a reddish glare, as if of some monstrous burning. But the color was not right for a fire. Not exactly.

"A city?" asked Babs breathlessly.

"A volcano," Cochrane told her. "I've staged shows that pretended to show intelligent creatures on other planets—funny how we've been dreaming of such things, back on Earth—but it isn't likely. Not since we've actually reached the stars."

"Why since then?"

"Because," said Cochrane, half ironically, "man was given dominion over all created things. I don't think we'll find rivals for that dominion. I can't imagine we'll find another race of creatures who could be—persons. Heaven

89

knows we try to rob each other of dignity, but I don't think there's another race to humiliate us when we find them!"

After a moment he added:

"Bad enough that we're here because there are deodorants and cosmetics and dog-foods and such things that people want to advertise to each other! We wouldn't be here but for them, and for the fact that some people are neurotics and some don't like their bosses and some are crazy in other fashions."

"Some crazinesses aren't bad," argued Babs.

"I've made a living out of them," agreed Cochrane sourly. "But I don't like them. I have a feeling that I could arrange things better. I know I couldn't, but I'd like to try. In my own small way, I'm even trying."

Babs chuckled.

"That's because you are a man. Women aren't so foolish. We're realists. We like creation—even men—the way creation is."

"I don't," Cochrane said irritably. "We've accomplished something terrific, and I don't get a kick out of it! My head is full of business details that have to be attended to tomorrow. I ought to be uplifted. I ought to be gloating! I ought to be happy! But I'm worrying for fear that this infernal planet is going to disappoint our audience!"

Babs chuckled again. Then she went to the stair leading to the compartment below.

"What's the matter?" he demanded.

"After all, I'm going to leave you alone," said Babs cheerfully. "You're always very careful not to talk to me in any personal fashion. I think you're afraid I'll tell you something for your own good. If I stayed here, I might. Goodnight!"

She started down the stairs. Cochrane said vexedly:

"Hold on! Confound it, I didn't know I was so transparent! I'm sorry, Babs. Look! Tell me something for my own good!"

Babs hesitated, and then said very cheerfully:

"You only see things the way a man sees them. This show, this trip—this whole business doesn't thrill you because you don't see it the way a woman would."

"Such as how? What does a woman see that I don't?"

"A woman," said Babs, "sees this planet as a place that men and women will come to live on. To live on! You

90

don't. You miss all the real implications of people actually living here. But they're the things a woman sees first of all."

Cochrane frowned.

"I'm not so conceited I can't listen to somebody else. If you've got an idea——"

"Not an idea," said Babs. "Just a reaction. And you can't explain a reaction to somebody who hasn't had it. Goodnight!"

She vanished down the stairs. Some time later, Cochrane heard the extremely minute sound of a door closing on one of the cabins three decks down in the space-ship.

He went back to his restless inspection of the night outside. He tried to make sense of what Babs had said. He failed altogether. In the end he settled in one of the over-elaborately cushioned chairs that had made this ship so attractive to deluded investors. He intended to think out what Babs might have meant. She was, after all, the most competent secretary he'd ever had, and he'd been wryly aware of how helpless he would be without her. Now he tried painstakingly to imagine what changes in one's view the inclusion of women among pioneers would involve. He worked out some seemingly valid points. But it was not a congenial mental occupation.

He fell asleep without realizing it, and was waked by the sound of voices all about him. It was morning again, and Johnny Simms was shouting boyishly at something he saw outside.

"Get at it, boy!" he cried enthusiastically. "Grab him! That's the way——"

Cochrane opened his eyes. Johnny Simms gazed out and down from a blister-port, waving his arms. His wife Alicia looked out of the same port without seeming to share his excited approval. Bell had dragged a camera across the control-room and was in the act of focussing it through a particular window.

"What's the matter?" demanded Cochrane.

He struggled out of his chair. And Johnny Simms' pleasure evaporated abruptly. He swore nastily, viciously, at something outside the ship. His wife touched his arm and spoke to him in a low tone. He turned furiously upon her, mouthing foulnesses.

Cochrane was formidably beside him, and Johnny Simms' expression of fury smoothed out instantly. He looked pleasant and amiable.

"The fight stopped," he explained offhandedly. "It was a good fight. But one of the creatures wouldn't stay and take his licking."

Alicia said steadily:

"There were some animals there. They looked rather like bears, only they had enormous ears."

Cochrane looked at Johnny Simms with hot eyes. It was absurd to be so chivalrous, perhaps, but he was enraged. After an instant he turned away and went to the port. The burned-over area was now only ashes. At its edge, charcoal showed. And now he could see trees and brushwood on beyond. The trees did not seem strange, because no trees would have seemed familiar. The brush did not impress him as exotic, because his experience with actual plants was restricted to the artificial plants on television sets and the artificially arranged plants on rooftops. He hardly let his eyes dwell on the vegetation at all. He searched for movement. He saw the moving furry rumps of half a dozen unknown creatures as they dived into concealment as if they had been frightened. He looked down and could see the hull of the ship and two of the three take-off fins on which it rested.

The airlock door was opening out. It swung wide. It swung back against the hull.

"Holden's making some sort of test of the air," Cochrane said shortly. "The animals were scared when the outside door swung open. I'll see what he finds out."

He hurried down. He found Babs standing beside the inner door of the airlock. She looked somehow pale. There were two saucers of greenish soup-like stuff on the floor at her feet. That would be, of course, the algae from the air-purifying-system tanks.

"The algae were alive," said Babs. "Dr. Holden went in the lock to try the air himself. He said he'd be very careful."

For some obscure reason Cochrane felt ashamed. There was a long, a desperately long wait. Then sounds of machinery. The outer door closing. Small whistlings—compressed air.

The inner door opened. Bill Holden came out of the lock, his expression zestfully surprised.

"Hello, Jed! I tried the air. It's all right! At a guess, maybe a little high in oxygen. But it feels wonderfully good to breathe! And I can report that the trees are wood
92

and the green is chlorophyl, and this is an Earth-type planet. That little smoky smell about is completely familiar—and I'm taking that as an analysis. I'm going to take a walk."

Cochrane found himself watching Babs' face. She looked enormously relieved, but even Cochrane—who was looking for something of the sort without realizing it—could not read anything but relief in her expression. She did not, for example, look admiring.

"I'll borrow one of Johnny Simms' guns," said Holden, "and take a look around. It's either perfectly safe or we're all dead anyhow. Frankly, I think it's safe. It feels right outside, Jed! It honestly feels right!"

"I'll come with you," said Cochrane. "Jones and the pilot are necessary if the ship's to get back to Earth. But we're expendable."

He went back to the control-room. Johnny Simms zestfully undertook to outfit them with arms. He made no proposal to accompany them. In twenty minutes or so, Cochrane and Holden went into the airlock and the door closed. A light came on automatically, precisely like the light in an electric refrigerator. Cochrane found his lips twitching a little as the analogy came to him. Seconds later the outer door opened, and they gazed down among the branches of tall trees. Cochrane winced. There was no railing and the height bothered him. But Holden swung out the sling. He and Cochrane descended, dangling, down fifty feet of unscarred, shining, metal hull.

The ground was still hot underfoot. Holden cast off the sling and moved toward cooler territory with an undignified haste. Cochrane followed him.

The smells were absolutely commonplace. Scorched wood. Smokiness. There were noises. Occasional cracklings from burned tree-trunks not wholly consumed. High-pitched, shrill musical notes. And in and among the smells there was an astonishing freshness in the feel of the air. Cochrane was especially apt to notice it because he had lived in a city back on Earth, and had spent four days in the moon-rocket, and then had breathed the Lunar City air for eighteen days more and had just come from the space-ship whose air was distinctly of the canned variety.

He did not notice the noise of the sling again in motion behind him. He was all eyes and ears and acute awareness of the completely strange environment. He was the more conscious of a general strangeness because he was so completely an urban product. Yet he and Holden were vastly less aware of the real strangeness about them than men of previous generations would have been. They did not notice the oddity of croaking sounds, like frogs, coming from the tree-tops. When they had threaded their way among leaning charred poles and came to green stuff underfoot and merely toasted foliage all around, Cochrane heard a sweet, high-pitched trilling which came from a half-inch hole in the ground. But he was not astonished by the place from which the trilling came. He was astonished at the sound itself.

There was a cry behind them.

"Mr. Cochrane! Doctor Holden!"

They swung about. And there was Babs on the ground, just disentangling herself from the sling. She had followed them out, after waiting until they had left the airlock and could not protest.

Cochrane swore to himself. But when Babs joined them breathlessly, after a hopping run over the hot ground, he said only:

"Fancy meeting you here!"

"I—I couldn't resist it," said Babs in breathless apology. "And you do have guns. It's safe enough—oh, look!"

She stared at a bush which was covered with pale purple flowers. Small creatures hovered in the air about it. She approached it and exclaimed again at the sweetness of its scent. Cochrane and Holden joined her in admiration.

In a sense they were foolishly unwary. This was completely strange territory. It could have contained anything. Earlier explorers would have approached every bush with caution and moved over every hilltop with suspicion, anticipating deadly creatures, unparalleled monsters, and exotic and peculiar circumstances designed to entrap the unprepared. Earlier explorers, of course, would probably have had advice from famous men to prepare them for all possible danger.

But this was a valley between snow-clad mountains. The river that ran down its length was fed by glaciers. This was a temperate climate. The trees were either coniferous or something similar, and the vegetation grew well but not with the frenzy of a tropic region. There were fruits here and there. Later, to be sure, they would prove to be mostly astringent and unpalatable. They were

94

broad-leafed, low-growing plants which would eventually turn out to be possessed of soft-fleshed roots which were almost unanimously useless for human purposes. There were even some plants with thorns and spines upon them. But they encountered no danger.

By and large, wild animals everywhere are ferocious only when desperate. No natural setting can permanently be so deadly that human beings will be attacked immediately they appear. An area in which peril is continuous is one in which there is so much killing that there is no food-supply left to maintain its predators. On the whole, there is simply a limit to how dangerous any place can be. Dangerous beasts have to be relatively rare, or they will not have enough to eat; then they will thin out until they are relatively rare and do have enough to eat.

So the three explorers moved safely, though their boldness was that of ignorance, below gigantic trees nearly as tall as the space-ship standing on end. They saw a small furry biped, some twelve inches tall, which waddled insanely in the exact line of their progress and with no apparent hope of outdistancing them. They saw a gauzy creature with incredibly spindly legs. It flew from one tree-trunk to another, clinging to rough bark on each in turn. Once they came upon a small animal which looked at them with enormous, panic-stricken blue eyes and then fled with a sinuous gait on legs so short that they seemed mere flippers. It dived into a hole and vanished.

But they came out to clear space. They could look for miles and miles. There was a savannah of rolling soil which gradually sloped down to a swift-running river. The grass—if it was grass—was quite green, but it had multitudes of tiny rose-colored flowers down the central rib of each leaf. Nearby it seemed the color of Earth-grass, but it faded imperceptibly into an incredible old-rose tint in the distance. The mountain-scarps on either side of the valley were sheer and tall. There was a great stony spur reaching out above the lowland, and there was forest at its top and bare brown stone dropping two thousand feet sheer. And up the valley, where it narrowed, a waterfall leaped out from the cliff and dropped hundreds of feet in an arc of purest white, until it was lost to view behind tree-tops.

They looked. They stared. Cochrane was a television producer, and Holden was a psychiatrist, and Babs was a

95

highly efficient secretary. They did not make scientific observations. The ecological system of the valley escaped their notice. They weren't qualified to observe that the flying things around seemed mostly to be furry instead of feathered, and that insects seemed few and huge and fragile, and they did not notice that most of the plants appeared to be deciduous, so indicating that this planet had pronounced seasons. But Holden said:

"Up in Greenland there's a hospital on a cliff like that. People with delusions of grandeur sometimes get cured just by looking at something that's so much greater and more splendid than they are. I'd like to see a hospital up yonder!"

Babs said, shining-eyed:

"A city could be built in this valley. Not a tall city, with gray streets and gardens on the roofs. This could be a nice little city like people used to have. There would be little houses, all separate, and there'd be grass all around and people could pluck flowers if they wanted to, to take inside ... There could be families here, and homes—not living-quarters!"

Cochrane said nothing. He was envious of the others. They saw, and they dreamed according to their natures. Cochrane somehow felt forlorn. Presently he said depressedly:

"We'll go back to the ship. You can work out your woman's viewpoint stuff with Bell, Babs. He'll write it, or you can give it to Alicia to put over when we go on the air."

Babs made no reply. The absence of comment was almost pointed. Cochrane realized that she wouldn't do it, though he couldn't see why.

They did go back to the ship. Cochrane sent Babs and Holden up the sling, first, while he waited down below. It was a singular sensation to stand there. He was the only human being afoot on a planet the size of Earth or larger, at the foot of a cliff of metal which was the space-ship's hull. He had a weapon in his hand, and it should defend him from anything. But he felt very lonely.

The sling came down for him. He felt sick at heart as it lifted him. He had an overwhelming conviction of incompetence, though he could not detail the reasons. The rope hauled him up, swaying, to the dizzy height of the airlock door. He could not feel elated. He was partly responsible for humankind's greatest achievement to date. But he had not quite the viewpoint that would let him enjoy its contemplation.

The ground quivered very faintly as he rose. It was not an earthquake. It was merely a temblor, such as anyone would expect to feel occasionally with six smoking volcanic cones in view. The green stuff all around was proof that it could be disregarded.

CHAPTER SEVEN

In the United States, some two-hundred-odd light-years away, it happened to be Tuesday. On this Tuesday, the broadcast from the stars was sponsored by Harvey's, the national men's clothing chain. Harvey's advertising department preferred discussion-type shows, because differences of opinion in the shows proper led so neatly into their tag-line. "You can disagree about anything but the quality of a Harvey suit! That's Superb!"

Therefore the broadcast after the landing of the ship on the volcanic planet was partly commercial, and partly pictures and reports from the Spaceways expedition, and partly queries and comments by big-name individuals on Earth. Inevitably there was Dabney. And Dabney was neurotic.

He did his best to make a shambles of everything.

The show started promptly enough at the beginning. There was a two-minute film-strip of business-suited puppets marching row on row, indicating the enormous popularity of Harvey's suits. Then a fast minute hill-billy puppet-show about two feuding mountaineers who found they couldn't possibly retain their enmity when they found themselves in agreement on the quality of Harvey suits. "That's Superb!" The commercial ended with a choral dance of madly enthusiastic miniature figures, dancing while they lustily sang the theme-song, "You can disagree, yes siree, you can disagree, About anything, indeed everything, you and me, But you can't, no you can't disagree, About the strictly super, extra super, Qualitee of a Harve-e-e-e suit! That's superb!"

And thereupon the television audience of several continents saw the faded-in image of mankind's first starship, poised upon its landing-fins among trees more splendid than even television shows had ever pictured before. The camera panned slowly, and showed such open spaces as very few humans had ever seen unencumbered by buildings, and mountains of a grandeur difficult for most people to believe in.

The scene cut to the space-ship's control-room and Al the pilot acted briskly as the leader of an exploration-party just returned—though he actually hadn't left the ship. He introduced Jamison, wearing improvised leggings and other trappings appropriate to an explorer in wilderness. Jamison began to extrapolate from his observations out the control-room port, adding film-clips for authority.

Smoothly and hypnotically, he pictured the valley as the ship descended the last few thousand feet, and told of the human colony to be founded in this vast and hospitable area just explored. Mountainside hotels for star-tourists would look down upon a scene of tranquility and cozy spaciousness. This would be the first human outpost in the stars. In the other valleys of this magnificent world there would be pasture-lands, and humankind would again begin to regard meat as a normal and not-extravagant part of its diet—on this planet, certainly! There were minerals beyond doubt, and water-power. The estimate was that at least the equivalent of the Asian continent had been made available for human occupation. And this splendid addition to the resources of humanity . . .

The second commercial cut Jamison off. Naturally. The sponsor was paying for time. So for Jamison was substituted the other fiction about the poor young man who found himself envied by the board of directors of the firm which employed him. His impeccable attire caused him to be promoted to vice-president without any question of whether or not he could fill the job. Because, of course, he wore a Harvey suit.

Alicia Keith showed herself on the screen and gave the woman's viewpoint as written about by Bell. She talked pleasantly about how it felt to move about on a planet never before trodden by human beings. She was interrupted by the pictured face of the lady editor of Joint Networks' feminine programs, who asked sweetly:

"Tell me, Alicia, what do you think the attainment of the stars will mean to the Average American housewife in the immediate future? Right now?"

Then Dabney came on. His appearance was fitted into the sequence from Lunar City, and his gestures were extravagant as anybody's gestures will be where their hands and arms weigh so small a fraction of Earth-normal.

"I wish," said Dabney impressively, "to congratulate the men who have so swiftly adapted my discovery of faster-than-light travel to practical use. I am overwhelmed at having been able to achieve a scientific triumph which in time will mean that mankind's future stretches endlessly and splendidly into the future!"

Here there was canned applause. Dabney held up his hand for attention. He thought. Visibly.

"But," he said urgently, "I admit that I am disturbed by the precipitancy of the action that has been taken. I feel as if I were like some powerful djinni giving gifts which the recipients may use without thought."

More canned applause, inserted because he had given instructions for it whenever he paused. The communicator-operator at Luna City took pleasure in following instructions exactly. Dabney held up his hand again. Again he performed feats of meditation in plain view.

"At the moment," he said anxiously, "as the author of this truly magnificent achievement, I have to use the same intellect which produced it, to examine the possibility of its ill-advised use. May not explorers—who took off without my having examined their plans and precautions— may not over-hasty users of my gift to humanity do harm? May they not find bacteria the human body cannot resist? May they not bring back plagues and epidemics? Have they prepared themselves to use my discovery only for the benefit of mankind? Or have they been precipitous? I shall have to apply myself to the devising of methods by which my discovery—made so that Humanity might attain hitherto undreamed-of-heights—I shall have to devise means by which it will be truly a blessing to mankind!"

Dabney, of course, had tasted the limelight. All the world considered him the greatest scientist of all time— except, of course, the people who knew something about science. But the first actual voyagers in space had become immediately greater heroes than himself. It was intolerable to Dabney to be restricted to taking bows on programs in which they starred. So he wrote a star part for himself.

The bearded biologist who followed him was to have lectured on the pictures and reports forwarded to him beforehand. But he could not ignore so promising a lead to show how much he knew. So he lectured authoritatively on the danger of extra-terrestrial disease-producing organisms being introduced on Earth. He painted a lurid picture, quoting from the history of pre-sanitation epidem-

100

ics. He wound up with a specific prophecy of something like the Black Death of the middle ages as lurking among the stars to decimate humanity. He was a victim of the well-known authority-trauma which affects some people on television when they think millions of other people are listening to them. They depart madly from their scripts to try to say something startling enough to justify all the attention they're getting.

The broadcast ended with a sentimental live commercial in which a dazzlingly beautiful girl melted into the arms of the worthy young man she had previously scorned. She found him irresistible when she noticed that he was wearing a suit she instantly knew by its quality could only come from Harvey's.

On the planet of glaciers and volcanoes, Holden fumed.

"Dammit!" he protested. "They talk like we're lepers! Like if we ever come back we'll be carriers of some monstrous disease that will wipe out the human race! As a matter of fact, we're no more likely to catch an extraterrestrial disease then to catch wry-neck from sick chickens!"

"That broadcast's nothing to worry about," said Cochrane.

"But it is!" insisted Holden. "Dabney and that fool biologist presented space-travel as a reason for panic! They could have every human being on Earth scared to death we'll bring back germs and everybody'll die of the roup!"

Cochrane grinned.

"Good publicity—if we needed it! Actually, they've boosted the show. From now on every presentation has a dramatic kick it didn't have before. Now everybody will feel suspense waiting for the next show. Has Jamison got the Purple Death on the Planet of Smoky Hilltops? Will darling Alicia Keith break out in green spots next time we watch her on the air? Has Captain Al of the star-roving space-ship breathed in spores of the Swelling Fungus? Are the space-travellers doomed? Tune in on our next broadcast and see! My dear Bill, if we weren't signed up for sponsors' fees, I'd raise our prices after this trick!"

Holden looked unconvinced. Cochrane said kindly:

"Don't worry! I could turn off the panic tomorrow—as much panic as there is. Kursten, Kasten, Hopkins and Fallowe had a proposal they set great store by. They wanted to parcel out a big contest for a name for mankind's second planet. They had regional sponsors lined up. It would have been worldwide! Advertisers were drooling over the prospect of people proposing names for this planet on box-tops! They were planning five million prize-money—and who'd be afraid of us then? But I turned it down because we haven't got a helicopter. We couldn't stage enough different shows from this planet to keep it going the minimum six weeks for a contest like that. Instead, we're taking off in a couple of hours. Jones agrees. The astronomers back home have picked out another Sol-type star that ought to have planets. We're going to run over and see what pickings we can find. Not too far—only twenty-some light-years!"

He regarded Holden quizzically to see how the last phases affected him. Holden didn't notice it.

"A contest—It doesn't make sense!"

"I know it isn't sense!" said Cochrane. "It's public-relations! I'm beginning to get my self-respect back. I see now that a space-exploration job is only as good as its public-relations man!"

He went zestfully to find Babs to tell her to leave the communicator-set and let queries go unanswered as a matter of simple business policy.

The sling which swung out of the airlock now became busy. They had landed on this planet, and they were going to leave it, and there had been a minimum of actual contact with its soil. So Jamison took his leggings—put on for the show—and he and Bell went down to the ground and foraged through the woods. Jamison carried one of Johnny Simms' guns, which he regarded with acute suspicion, and Bell carried cameras. They photographed trees and underbrush, first as atmosphere and then with fanatic attention to leaves and fruits or flowers. Bell got pictures of one of the small, furry bipeds that Cochrane and Holden had spied when Babs was with them. He got a picture of what he believed to be a spider-web—it was thicker and heavier and huger than any web on Earth—and rather fearfully looked for the monster that could string thirty-foot cables as thick as fishing-twine. Then he found that it was not a snare at all. It was a construction at whose center something undiscoverable had made a nest, with eggs in it. Some creature had made an unapproachable home for itself where its young would not be assailed by predators.

Al, the pilot, went out of the lock and descended to the ground and went as far as the edge of the ash-ring. But he did not go any farther. He wandered about unhappily, pretending that he did not want to go into the woods. He tried to appear quite content to view half-burnt trees for his experience of the first extra-terrestrial planet on which men had landed. He did kick up some pebbles—water-rounded—and one of them had flecks of what looked like gold in it. Al regarded it excitedly, and then thought of freight-rates. But he did scrabble for more. Presently he had a pocket-full of small stones which would be regarded with rapture by his nieces and nephews because they had come from the stars. Actually, they were quite common-place minerals. The flecks of what looked like gold were only iron pyrates.

Jones did not leave the ship. He was puttering. Nor Alicia. Holden urged her to take a walk, and she said quietly:

"Johnny's out with a gun. He's hunting. I don't like to be with Johnny when he may be disappointed."

She smiled, and Holden sourly went away. There had been no particular consequences of Johnny Simms' inability to remember what was right and what was wrong. But Holden felt like a normal man about men whose wives look patient. Even psychiatrists feel that it is somehow disreputable to illtreat a woman who doesn't fight back. This attitude is instinctive. It is what is called the fine, deep-rooted impulse to chivalry which is one of the prides of modern culture.

Holden settled dourly down at the communicator to get an outgoing call to Earth, when there were some hundreds of incoming calls backed up. By sheer obstinacy and bad manners he made it. He got a connection to a hospital where he was known, and he talked to its bacteriologist. The bacteriologist was competent, but not yet famous. With Holden giving honest guesses at the color of the sunlight, and its probable ultra-violet content, and with careful estimates of the exactness with which burning vegetation here smelled like Earth-plants, they arrived at imprecise but common sense conclusions. Of the hundreds of thousands of possible organic compounds, only so many actually took part in the life-processes of creatures on Earth. Yet there were hundreds of thousands of species prepared to make use of anything usable. If the sunlight and temperature of the two worlds were similar, it was somewhat more than likely that the same chemical compounds would be used by living things on both. So that there could be micro-organisms on the new planet which could be harmful. But on the other hand, either they would be familiar in the toxins they produced—and human bodies could resist them—or else they would be new compounds to which humans would react allergically. Basically, then, if anybody on the ship developed hives, they had reason to be frightened. But so long as nobody sneezed or broke out in welts, their lives were probably safe.

This comforting conclusion took a long time to work out. Meanwhile Babs and Cochrane had swung down to the ground and gone hiking. Cochrane was armed as before, though he had no experience as a marksman. In television shows he had directed the firing of weapons shooting blank charges—cut to a minimum so they wouldn't blast the mikes. He knew what motions to go through, but nothing else.

They did not explore in the same direction as their first excursion. The ship was to take off presently, as soon as this planet had turned enough for the space-ship's nose to point nearly in the direction of their next target. They had two hours for exploration.

They came upon something which lay still across their path, like a great serpent. Cochrane looked at it startledly. Then he saw that the round, glistening seeming snake was fastened to the ground by rootlets. It was a plant which grew like a creeper, absorbing nourishment from a vast root-area. Somewhere, no doubt, it would rear upward and spread out leaves to absorb the sun's light. It used, in a way, the principle of those lateral wells which in dry climates gather water too scarce to collect in merely vertical holes.

They went on and on, admiring and amazed. All about them were curiosities of adaptation, freaks of ecological adjustment, marvels of symbiotic cooperation. A botanist would have swooned with joy at the material all about. A biologist would have babbled happily. Babs and Cochrane admired without information. They walked interestedly but unawed among the unparalleled. Back on Earth they knew as much as most people about nature—practically nothing at all. Babs had never seen any wild plants before. She was fascinated by what she saw, and exclaimed at everything. But she did not realize a fraction of the marvels on which her eyes rested. On the whole, she survived.

"It's a pity we haven't got a helicopter," Cochrane said

regretfully. "If we could fly around from place to place, and send back pictures ... We can't do it in the ship ... It would burn more fuel than we've got."

Babs wrinkled her forehead.

"Doctor Holden's badly worried because we can't make as alluring a picture as he'd like."

Cochrane halted, to watch something which was flat like a disk of gray-green flesh and which moved slowly out of their path with disquieting writhing motions. It vanished, and he said:

"Yes. Bill's an honest man, even if he is a psychiatrist. He wants desperately to do something for the poor devils back home who're so pitifully frustrated. There are tens of millions of men who can't hope for anything better than to keep the food and shelter supply intact for themselves and their families. They can't even pretend to hope for more than that. There isn't more than so much to go around. But Bill wants to give them hope. He figures that without hope the world will turn madhouse in another generation. It will."

"You're trying to do something about that!" said Babs quickly. "Don't you think you're offering hope to everybody back on Earth?"

"No!" snapped Cochrane. "I'm not trying anything so abstract as furnishing hope to a frustrated humanity! Nobody can supply an abstraction! Nobody can accomplish an abstraction! Everything that's actually done is specific and real! Maybe you can find abstract qualities in it after it's done, but I'm a practical man! I'm not trying to produce an improved psychological climate, suitable for debilitated psychos! I'm trying to get a job done!"

"I've wondered," admitted Babs, "what the job is."

Cochrane grimaced.

"You wouldn't believe it, Babs."

There was an odd quivering underfoot. Trees shook. There was no other peculiarity anywhere. Nothing fell. No rocks rolled. In a valley among volcanoes, where the smoke from no less than six cones could be seen at once, temblors would not do damage. What damage mild shakings could do would have been done centuries since.

Babs said uneasily:

"That feels—queer, doesn't it?"

Cochrane nodded. But just as he and Babs had never been conditioned to be afraid of animals, they had been conditioned by air-travel at home and space-travel to here against alarm at movements of their surroundings. Temblors were evidently frequent at this place. Trees were anchored against them as against prevailing winds in exposed situations. Landslides did not remain poised to fall. Really unstable slopes had been shaken down long ago.

"I wish we had a helicopter," Cochrane repeated. "The look of the mountains as we came down, with glaciers between the smoking cones—that was good show-stuff! We could have held interest here until we worked that naming contest. We could use the extra capital that would bring in! As it is, we've got to move on with practically nothing accomplished. The trouble is that I didn't think we would succeed as we have! Heaven knows I could have gotten helicopters!"

He helped her up a small steep incline, where rock protruded from a hillside.

The ground trembled again. Not alarmingly, but Babs' hold of his hand tightened a little. They continued to climb. They came out atop a small bare prominence which rose above the forest. Here they could see over the treetops in a truly extensive view. The mountains all about were clearly visible. Some were ten and some twenty miles away. Some, still farther, were barely visible in the thin haze of distance. But there was a thick pall of smoke hovering about one of the farthest. It was mushroom-shaped. At one time in human history, it would have seemed typically a volcanic cloud. To Cochrane and Babs, it was typically the cloud of an atomic explosion.

The ground shook sharply underfoot. Babs staggered.

Flying things rose from the forests in swarms. They hovered and darted and flapped above the tree-tops. Temblors did not alarm the creatures of the valley. But groundshocks like this last were another matter.

A great tree, rearing above its fellows, toppled slowly. With ripping, tearing noises, it bent sedately toward the smoking, far-away mountain. It crashed thunderously down upon smaller trees. There were other rending noises. The flying things rose higher, seeming agitated. Echoes sounded in the ears of the two atop the hill.

There was another sharp shock. Babs gave a little, inarticulate cry. She pointed.

There was much smoke in the distance. Over the faraway cone, which was indistinct in the smoke of its own making—over the edge of the distant mountains a glare appeared. It was a thin line of bright white light. With infinite deliberation it began to creep down the slanting, blessedly remote mountainside.

The ground seemed to shift abruptly, and then shift back. Across and down the valley, five miles away, a portion of the stony wall detached itself and slid downward in seeming slow motion. Two more great trees made ripping sounds. One crashed. There was an enormous darkness above one part of the sky. Its under side glowed from fires as of hell, in the crater beneath it. There were sparkings above the mountaintop.

Very oddly indeed, the sky overhead was peacefully blue. But at the horizon a sheet of fire rolled down mile-long slopes. It seemed to move with infinite deliberation, but to move visibly at such a distance it must have been traveling like an express-train. It must have been unthinkably hot, glaring-white molten stone, thin as water, pouring downward in a flood of fire.

There was no longer a sensation of the ground trembling underfoot. Now the noticeable sensation was when the ground was still. Temblors were practically continuous. There were distinct sharp impacts, as of violent blows nearby.

Babs stared, fascinated. She glanced up at Cochrane. His skin was white. There were beads of sweat on his forehead.

"We're safe here, aren't we?" she asked, scared.

"I think so. But I'm not going to take you through falling trees while this is going on! There's another tree down! I'm worrying about the ship! If it topples——."

She looked at the nose of the space-ship, gleaming silver metal, rising from the trees about the landing-spot it had burned clear. A third of its length was visible.

"If it topples," said Cochrane, "we'll never be able to take off. It has to point up to lift."

Babs looked from the ship to him, and back again. Then her eyes went fearfully to the remote mountain. Rumblings came from it now. They were not loud. They were hardly more than dull growlings, at the lower limit of audible pitch. They were like faint and distant thunder. There were flashings like lightning in the cloud which now enveloped the mountain's top.

Cochrane made an indescribable small sound. He stared at the ship. As explosion-waves passed over the ground, a faint, unanimous movement of the treetops became visible.

It seemed to Cochrane that the space-ship wavered as if about to fall from its upright position.

It was not designed to stand such violence as a fall would imply. Its hull would be dented or rent. It was at least possible that its fuel-store would detonate. But even if its fall were checked by still-standing trees about it, it could never take off again. The eight humans of its company could never juggle it back to a vertical position. Rocket-thrust would merely push it in the direction its nose pointed. Toppled, its rocket-thrust would merely shove it blindly over stones and trees and to destruction.

The ship swayed again. Visibly. Ground-waves made its weight have the effect of blows. Part of its foundation rested on almost-visible stone, only feet below the ground-level. But one of the landing-fins rested on humus. As the shocks passed, that fin-foot sank into the soft soil. The space-ship leaned perceptibly.

Flying creatures darted back and forth above the tree-tops. Miles away, insensate violence reigned. Clouds of dust and smoke shot miles into the air, and half a mountainside glowed white-hot, and there was the sound of long-continued thunder, and the ground shook and quivered . . .

There were movements nearby. A creature with yellow fur and the shape of a bear with huge ears came padding out of the forest. It swarmed up the bare stone of the hill on which Babs and Cochrane stood.

It ignored them. Halfway up the unwooded part of the hill, it stopped and made plaintive, high-pitched noises. Other creatures came. Many had come while the man and girl were too absorbed to notice. Now two more of the large animals came out into the open and climbed the hill.

Babs said shakily:

"Do you—think they'll—do you think—"

There was a nearer roaring. The space-ship leaned, and leaned . . . Cochrane's lips tensed.

The space-ship's rockets bellowed and a storm of hurtling smoke flashed up around it. It lifted, staggering as its steering-jets tried frantically to swing its lower parts underneath its mass. It lurched violently, and the rockets flamed terribly. It lifted again. Its tail was higher than the trees, but it did not point straight up. It surged horribly across the top of the forest, leaving a vast flash of flaming vegetation behind it. Then it steadied, and aimed skyward and climbed . . .

Then it was not. Obviously the Dabney field booster

had been flashed on to get the ship out to space. The ship had vanished into emptiness.

The Dabney field had flicked it some hundred and seventy-odd light-years from Earth's moon in the flicker of a heart-beat. It might have gone that far again. Whoever was in it had had no choice but to take off, and no way to take off without suicidal use of fuel in any other way.

Cochrane looked at where the ship had vanished. Seconds passed. There came the thunderclap of air closing the vacuum the ship's disappearance had left.

There were squealings behind the pair on the hilltop. Eight of the huge yellow beasts were out in the open, now. Tiny, furry biped animals waddled desperately to get out of their way. Smaller creatures scuttled here and there. A sinuous creature with fur but no apparent legs writhed its way upward. But all the creatures were frightened. They observed an absolute truce, under the overmastering greater fear of nature.

Far away, the volcano on the skyline boomed and flashed and emitted monstrous clouds of smoke. The shining, incandescent lava on its flanks glared across the glaciers.

Babs gasped suddenly. She realized the situation in which she and Cochrane had been left.

Shivering, she pressed close to him as the distant black smoke-cloud spread toward the center of the sky.

CHAPTER EIGHT

BEFORE SUNSET, THEY REACHED THE AREA OF ASHES where the ship had stood. Cochrane was sure that if anybody else had been left besides themselves, the landing-place was an inevitable rendezvous. Only three members of the ship's company had been inside when Babs and Cochrane left to stroll for the two hours astronomers on Earth had set as a waiting-period. Jones had been in the ship, and Holden, and Alicia Simms. Everybody else had been exploring. Their attitude had been exactly that of sight-seers and tourists. But they could have gotten back before the take-off.

Apparently they had. Nobody seemed to have returned to the burned-over space since the ship's departure. The blast of the rockets had erased all previous tracks, but still there was a thin layer of ash resettled over the clearing. Footprints would have been visible in it. Anybody remaining would have come here. Nobody had. Babs and Cochrane were left alone.

There were still temblors, but the sharper shocks no longer came. There was conflagration in the wood, where the lurching ship had left a long fresh streak of forest-fire. The two castaways stared at the round, empty landing-place. Overhead, the blue sky turned yellow—but where the smoke from the eruption rose, the sky early became a brownish red—and presently the yellow faded to gold. Unburned green foliage all about was singularly beautiful in that golden glow. But it was more beautiful still as the sky turned rose-pink and then carmine in turn, and then crimson from one horizon to the other save where the volcanic smoke-cloud marred the color. Then the east darkened, and became a red so deep as to be practically black, and unfamiliar bright stars began to peep through it.

Before darkness was complete, Cochrane dragged burning branches from the edge of the new fire—the heat was

110

searing—and built a new and smaller fire in the place where the ship had been.

"This isn't for warmth," he explained briefly, "but so we'll have light if we need it. And it isn't likely that animals will be anything but afraid of it."

He went off to drag charred masses of burnable stuff from the burned-out first forest fire. He built a sort of rampart in the very center of the clearing. He brought great heaps of scorched wood. He did not know how much was needed to keep the fire going until dawn.

When he finished, Babs was silently at work trying to find out how to keep the fire going. The burning parts had to be kept together. One branch, burning alone, died out. Two red-hot brands in contact kept each other alight.

"I'm sorry we haven't anything to eat," Cochrane told her.

"I'm not hungry," she assured him. "What are we going to do now?"

"There's nothing to do until morning," Unconsciously, Cochrane looked grim. "Then there'll be plenty. Food, for one thing. We don't know, actually, whether or not there's anything really edible on this planet—for us. It could be that there are fruits or possibly stalks or leaves that would be nourishing. Only—we don't know which is which. We have to be careful. We might pick something like poison ivy!"

Babs said:

"But the ship will come back!"

"Of course," agreed Cochrane. "But it may take them some time to find us. This is a pretty big planet, you know."

He estimated his supply of burnable stuff. He improved the rampart he had made at first. Babs stared at him. After four or five minutes he stepped back.

"You can lean against this," he explained. "You can watch the fire quite comfortably. And it's a sort of wall. The fire will light one side of you and the wall will feel comforting behind you when you get sleepy."

Babs nodded. She swallowed.

"I—think I see what you mean when you say they may have trouble finding us, because this planet is so large."

Cochrane nodded reluctantly.

"Of course there's this burned-off space for a marker," he observed cheerfully. "But it could take several days for them to see it."

Babs swallowed again. She said carefully:

"The—ship can't hover like a helicopter, to search. You said so. It doesn't have fuel enough. They can't really search for us at all! The only way to make a real search would be to go back to Earth and—bring back helicopters and fuel for them and men to fly them . . . Isn't that right?"

"Not necessarily. But we do have to figure on a matter of—well—two or three days as a possibility."

Babs moistened her lips and he said quickly:

"I did a show once about some miners lost in a wilderness. A period show. In it, they knew that part of their food was poisoned. They didn't know what. They had to have all their food. And of course they didn't have laboratories with which to test for poison."

Babs eyed him oddly.

"They bandaged their arms," said Cochrane, "and put scraps of the different foodstuffs under the bandages. The one that was poisonous showed. It affected the skin. Like an allergy-test. I'll try that trick in the morning when there's light to pick samples by. There are berries and stuff. There must be fruits. A few hours should test them."

Babs said without intonation:

"And we can watch what the animals eat."

Cochrane nodded gravely. Animals on Earth can live on things that—to put it mildly—humans do not find satisfying. Grass, for example. But it was good for Babs to think of cheering things right now. There would be plenty of discouragement to contemplate later.

There was a flicker of brightness in the sky. Presently the earth quivered. Something made a plaintive, "*waa-waa-waaaaa!*" sound off in the night. Something else made a noise like the tinkling of bells. There was an abstracted hooting presently, which now was nearby and now was far away, and once they heard something which was exactly like the noise of water running into a pool. But the source of that particular burbling moved through the dark wood beyond the clearing.

It was not wholly dark where they were, even aside from their own small fire. The burning trees in the departing ship's rocket-trail sent up a column of white which remaining flames illuminated. The remarkably primitive camp Cochrane had made looked like a camp on a tiny snow-field, because of the ashes.

"We've got to think about shelter," said Babs presently, very quietly indeed. "If there are glaciers, there must be
112

winter here. If there is winter, we have to find out which animals we can eat, and how to store them."

"Hold on!" protested Cochrane. "That's looking too far ahead!"

Babs clasped her hands together. It could have been to keep their trembling from being seen. Cochrane was regarding her face. She kept that under admirable control.

"Is it?" asked Babs. "On the broadcast Mr. Jamison said that there was as much land here as on all the continent of Asia. Maybe he exaggerated. Say there's only as much land not ice-covered as there is in South America. It's all forest and plain and uninhabited." She moistened her lips, but her voice was very steady. "If all of South America was uninhabited, and there were two people lost in it, and nobody knew where they were—how long would it take to find them?"

"It would be a matter of luck," admitted Cochrane.

"If the ship comes back, it can't hover to look for us. There isn't fuel enough. It couldn't spot us from space if it went in an orbit like a space platform. By the time they could get help—they wouldn't even be sure we were alive. If we can't count on being found right away, this burned-over place will be green again. In two or three weeks they couldn't find it anyhow."

Cochrane fidgeted. He had worked out all this for himself. He'd been disturbed at having to tell it, or even admit it to Babs. Now she said in a constrained voice:

"If men came to this planet and built a city and hunted for us, it might still be a hundred years before anybody happened to come into this valley. Looking for us would be worse than looking for a needle in a haystack. I don't think we're going to be found again."

Cochrane was silent. He felt guiltily relieved that he did not have to break this news to Babs. Most men have an instinctive feeling that a woman will blame them for bad news they hear.

A long time later, Babs said as quietly as before:

"Johnny Simms asked me to come along while he went hunting. I didn't. At least I—I'm not cast away with him!"

Cochrane said gruffly:

"Don't sit there and brood! Try to get some sleep."

She nodded. After a long while, her head drooped. She jerked awake again. Cochrane ordered her vexedly to make herself comfortable. She stretched out beside the wall of wood that Cochrane had made. She said quietly:

"While we're looking for food tomorrow morning, we'd better keep our eyes open for a place to build a house."

She closed her eyes.

Cochrane kept watch through the dark hours. He heard night-cries in the forest, and once toward dawn the distant volcano seemed to undergo a fresh paroxysm of activity. Boomings and explosions rumbled in the night. There were flickerings in the sky. But there were fewer temblors after it, and no shocks at all.

More than once, Cochrane found himself dozing. It was difficult to stay in a state of alarm. There was but one single outcry in the forest that sounded like the shriek of a creature seized by a carnivore. That was not nearby. He tried to make plans. He felt bitterly self-reproachful that he knew so few of the things that would be useful to a castaway. But he had been a city man all his life. Woodcraft was not only out of his experience—on overcrowded Earth it would have been completely useless.

From time to time he found himself thinking, instead of practical matters, of the astonishing sturdiness of spirit Babs displayed.

When she waked, well after daybreak, and sat up blinking, he said:

"Er—Babs. We're in this together. From now on, if you want to tell me something for my own good, go ahead! Right?"

She rubbed her eyes on her knuckles and said,

"I'd have done that anyhow. For both our good. Don't you think we'd better try to find a place where we can get a drink of water? Water has to be right to drink!"

They set off, Cochrane carrying the weapon he'd brought from the ship. It was Babs who pointed out that a stream should almost certainly be found where rain would descend, downhill. Babs, too, spotted one of the small, foot-high furry bipeds feasting gluttonously on small round objects that grew from the base of a small tree instead of on its branches. The tree, evidently, depended on four-footed rather than on flying creatures to scatter its seeds. They gathered samples of the fruit. Cochrane peeled a sliver of the meat from one of the round objects and put it under his watchstrap.

They found a stream. They found other fruits, and Cochrane prepared the same test for them as for the first. One of the samples turned his skin red and angry almost

114

immediately. He discarded it and all the fruits of the kind from which it came.

At midday they tasted the first-gathered fruit. The flesh was red and juicy. There was a texture it was satisfying to chew on. The taste was indeterminate save for a very mild flavor of maple and peppermint mixed together.

They had no symptoms of distress afterward. Other fruits were less satisfactory. Of the samples which the skin-test said were non-poisonous, one was acrid and astringent, and two others had no taste except that of greenness—practically the taste of any leaf one might chew.

"I suppose," said Cochrane wryly, as they headed back toward the ash-clearing at nightfall, "we've got to find out if the animals can be eaten."

Babs nodded matter-of-factly.

"Yes. Tonight I'm taking part of the watch. As you remarked this morning, we're in this together."

He looked at her sharply, and she flushed.

"I mean it!" she said doggedly. "I'm watching part of the night!"

He was desperately tired. His muscles were not yet back to normal after the low gravity on the moon. She'd had more rest than he. He had to let her help. But there was embarrassment between them because it looked as if they would have to spend the rest of their lives together, and they had not made the decision. It had been made for them. And they had not acknowledged it yet.

When they reached the clearing, Cochrane began to drag new logs toward the central place where much of last night's supply of fuel remained. Matter-of-factly, Babs began to haul stuff with him. He said vexedly:

"Quit it! I've already been realizing how little I know about the things we're going to need to survive! Let me fool myself about masculine strength, anyhow!"

She smiled at him, a very little. But she went obediently to the fire to experiment with cookery of the one palatable variety of fruit from this planet's trees. He drove himself to bring more wood than before. When he settled down she said absorbedly:

"Try this, Jed."

Then she flushed hotly because she'd inadvertently used his familiar name. But she extended something that was toasted and not too much burned. He ate, with weariness sweeping over him like a wave. The cooked fruit was almost a normal food, but it did need salt. There would be trouble finding salt on this planet. The water that should be in the seas was frozen in the glaciers. Salt would not have been leached out of the soil and gathered in the seas. It would be a serious problem. But Cochrane was very tired indeed.

"I'll take the first two hours," said Babs briskly. "Then I'll wake you."

He showed her how to use the weapon. He meant to let himself drift quietly off to sleep, acting as if he had a little trouble going off. But he didn't. He lay down, and the next thing he knew Babs was shaking him violently. In the first dazed instant when he opened his eyes he thought they were surrounded by forest fire. But it wasn't that. It was dawn, and Babs had let him sleep the whole night through, and the sky was golden-yellow from one horizon to the other. More, he heard the now-familiar cries of creatures in the forest. But also he heard a roaring sound, very thin and far away, which could only be one thing.

"Jed! Jed! Get up! Quick! The ship's coming back! The ship! We've got to move!"

She dragged him to his feet. He was suddenly wide-awake. He ran with her. He flung back his head and stared up as he ran. There was a pin-point of flame and vapor almost directly overhead. It grew swiftly in size. It plunged downward.

They reached the surrounding forest and plunged into it. Babs stumbled, and Cochrane caught her, and they ran onward hand in hand to get clear away from the down-blast of the rockets. The rocket-roaring grew louder and louder.

The castaways gazed. It was the ship. From below, fierce flames poured down, blue-white and raging. The silver hull slanted a little. It shifted its line of descent. It came down with a peculiar deftness of handling that Cochrane had not realized before. Its rockets splashed, but the flame did not extend out to the edge of the clearing that had been burned off at first. The rocket-flames, indeed, did not approach the proportion to be seen on rockets on film-tape, or as Cochrane had seen below the moon-rocket descending on Earth.

The ship settled within yards of its original landing-place. Its rockets dwindled, but remained burning. They dwindled again. The noise was outrageous, but still not the intolerable tumult of a moon-rocket landing on Earth.

116

The rockets cut off.

The airlock door opened. Cochrane and Babs waved cheerfully from the edge of the clearing. Holden appeared in the door and shouted down:

"Sorry to be so long coming back."

He waved and vanished. They had, of course, to wait until the ground at least partly cooled before the landing-sling could be used. Around them the noises of the forest continued. There were cooling, crackling sounds from the ship.

"I wonder how they found their way back?" said Babs. "I didn't think they ever could. Did you?"

"Babs," said Cochrane, "you lied to me! You said you'd wake me in two hours. But you let me sleep all night!"

"You'd let me sleep the night before," she told him composedly. "I was fresher than you were, and today'd have been a pretty bad one. We were going to try to kill some animals. You needed the rest."

Cochrane said slowly:

"I found out something, Babs. Why you could face things. Why we humans haven't all gone mad. I think I've gotten the woman's viewpoint now, Babs. I like it."

She inspected the looming blister-ports of the ship, now waiting for the ground to cool so they could come aboard.

"I think we'd have made out if the ship hadn't come," Cochrane told her. "We'd have had a woman's viewpoint to work from. Yours. You looked ahead to building a house. Of course you thought of finding food, but you were thinking of the possibility of winter and—building a house. You weren't thinking only of survival. You were thinking far ahead. Women must think farther ahead than men do!"

Babs looked at him briefly, and then returned to her apparently absorbed contemplation of the ship.

"That's what's the matter with people back on Earth," Cochrane said urgently. "There's no frustration as long as women can look ahead—far ahead, past here and now! When women can do that, they can keep men going. It's when there's nothing to plan for that men can't go on because women can't hope. You see? You saw a city here. A little city, with separate homes. On Earth, too many people can't think of more than living-quarters and keeping food enough for them—them only!—coming in. They can't hope for more. And it's when that happens—You see?"

Babs did not answer. Cochrane fumbled. He said angrily:

117

"Confound it, can't you see what I'm trying to say? We'd have been better off, as castaways, than back on Earth crowded and scared of our jobs! I'm saying I'd rather stay here with you than go back to the way I was living before we started off on this voyage! I think the two of us could make out under any circumstances! I don't want to try to make out without you! It isn't sense!" Then he scowled helplessly. "Dammit, I've staged plenty of shows in which a man asked a girl to marry him, and they were all phoney. It's different, now that *I* mean it! What's a good way to ask you to marry me?"

Babs looked momentarily up into his face. She smiled ever so faintly.

"They're watching us from the ports," she said. "If you want my viewpoint—If we were to wave to them that we'll be right back, we can get some more of those fruits I cooked. It might be interesting to have some to show them."

He scowled more deeply than before.

"I'm sorry you feel that way. But if that's it—"

"And on the way," said Babs. "When they're not watching, you might kiss me."

They had a considerable pile of the red-fleshed fruits ready when the ground had cooled enough for them to reach the landing-sling.

Once aboard the ship, Cochrane headed for the control-room, with Jamison and Bell tagging after him. Bell had an argument.

"But the volcano's calmed down—there's only a wall of steam where the lava hit the glaciers—and we could fix up a story in a couple of hours! I've got back-ground shots! You and Babs could make the story-scenes and we'd have a castaway story! Perfect! The first true castaway story from the stars—. You know what that would mean!"

Cochrane snarled at him.

"Try it and I'll tear you limb from limb! I've put enough of other people's private lives on the screen! My own stays off! I'm not going to have even a phoney screen-show built around Babs and me for people to gabble about!"

Bell said in an injured tone:

"I'm only trying to do a good job! I started off on this business as a writer. I haven't had a real chance to show what I can do with this sort of material!"

"Forget it!" Cochrane snapped again. "Stick to your cameras!"

Jamison said hopefully:

"You'll give me some data on plants and animals, Mr. Cochrane? Won't you? I'm doing a book with Bell's pictures, and—"

"Let me alone!" raged Cochrane.

He reached the control-room. Al, the pilot, sat at the controls with an air of special alertness.

"You're all right? For our lined up trip, we ought to leave in about twenty minutes. We'll be pointing just about right then."

"I'm all right," said Cochrane. "And you can take off when you please." To Jones he said: "How'd you find us? I didn't think it could be done."

"Doctor Holden figured it out," said Jones. "Simple enough, but I was lost! When the ground-shocks came, everybody else ran to the ship. We waited for you. You didn't come." It had been, of course, because Cochrane would not risk taking Babs through a forest in which trees were falling. "We finally had to choose between taking off and crashing. So we took off."

"That was quite right. We'd all be messed up if you hadn't," Cochrane told him.

Jones waved his hands.

"I didn't think we could ever find you again. We were sixty light-years away when that booster effect died out. Then Doctor Holden got on the communicator. He got Earth. The astronomers back there located us and gave us the line to get back by. We found the planet. Even then I didn't see how we'd pick out the valley. But Doc had had 'em checking the shots we transmitted as we were making our landing. We had the whole first approach on film-tape. They put a crowd of map-comparators to work. We went in a Space Platform orbit around the planet, transmitting what we saw from out there—they figured the orbit for us, too—and they checked what we transmitted against what we'd photographed going down. So they were able to spot the exact valley and tell us where to come down. We actually spotted this valley last night, but we couldn't land in the dark."

Cochrane felt abashed.

"I couldn't have done that job," he admitted, "so I didn't think anybody could. Hm. Didn't all this cost a lot of fuel?"

Jones actually smiled.

"I worked out something. We don't use as much fuel

119

as we did. We're probably using too much now. Al—go ahead and lift. I want to check what the new stuff does, anyhow. Take off!"

The pilot threw a switch, and Jones threw another, a newly installed one, just added to his improvised control-column. A light glowed brightly. Al pressed one button, very gently. A roaring set up outside. The ship started up. There was practically no feeling of acceleration, this time. The ship rose lightly. Even the rocket roar was mild indeed, compared to its take-off from Luna and the sound of its first landing on the planet just below.

Cochrane saw the valley floors recede, and mountain-walls drop below. From all directions, then, vegetation-filled valleys flowed toward the ship, and underneath. Glaciers appeared, and volcanic cones, and then enormous stretches of white, with smoking dots here and there upon it. In seconds, it seemed, the horizon was visibly curved. In other seconds the planet being left behind was a monstrous white ball, and there were patches of intolerable white sun-light coming in the ports.

And Cochrane felt queer. Jones had given the order for take-off. Jones had determined to leave at this moment, because Jones had tests he wanted to make . . . Cochrane felt like a passenger. From the man who decided things because he was the one who knew what had to be done, he had become something else. He had been absent two nights and part of a day, and decisions had been made in which he had no part—

It felt queer. It felt even startling.

"We're in a modification of the modified Dabney field now," observed Jones in a gratified tone. "You know the original theory."

"I don't," acknowledged Cochrane.

"The field's always a pipe, a tube, a column of stressed space between the field-plates," Jones reminded him. "When we landed the first time, back yonder, the tail of the ship wasn't in the field at all. The field stretched from the bow of the ship only, out to that last balloon we dropped. We were letting down at an angle to that line. It was like a kite and a string and the kite's tail. The string was the Dabney field, and the direction we were heading was the kite's tail."

Cochrane nodded. It occurred to him that Jones was very much unlike Dabney. Jones had discovered the Dab-ney field, but having sold the fame-rights to it, he now apparently thought "Dabney Field" was the proper technical term for his own discovery, even in his own mind.

"Back on the moon," Jones went on zestfully, "I wasn't sure that a field once established would hold in atmosphere. I hoped that with enough power I could keep it, but I wasn't sure—"

"This doesn't mean much to me, Jones," said Cochrane. "What does it add up to?"

"Why—the field held down into atmosphere. And we were out of the primary field as far as the tail of the ship was concerned. But this time we landed, I'd hooked in some ready-installed circuits. There was a second Dabney field from the stern of the ship to the bow. There was the main one, going out to those balloons and then back to Earth. But there was—and is—a second one only enclosing the ship. It's a sort of bubble. We can still trail a field behind us, and anybody can follow in any sort of ship that's put into it. But now the ship has a completely independent, second field. Its tail is never outside!"

Cochrane did not have the sort of mind to find such information either lucid or suggestive.

"So what happens?"

"We have both plates of a Dabney field always with us," said Jones triumphantly. "We're always in a field, even landing in atmosphere, and the ship has practically no mass even when it's letting down to landing. It has weight, but next to no mass. Didn't you notice the difference?"

"Stupid as it may seem, I didn't," admitted Cochrane. "I haven't the least idea what you're talking about."

Jones looked at him patiently.

"Now we can shoot our exhaust out of the field! The ship-field, not the main one!"

"I'm still numb," said Cochrane. "Multiple sclerosis of the brain-cells, I suppose. Let me just take your word for it."

Jones tried once more.

"Try to see it! Listen! When we landed the first time we had to use a lot of fuel because the tail of the ship wasn't in the Dabney field. It had mass. So we had to use a lot of rocket-power to slow down that mass. In the field, the ship hasn't much mass—the amount depends on the strength of the field—but rockets depend for their thrust on the mass that's thrown away astern. Looked at that way, rockets shouldn't push hard in a Dabney field. There

121

oughtn't to be any gain to be had by the field at all. You see?"

Cochrane fumbled in his head.

"Oh, yes. I thought of that. But there is an advantage. The ship does work."

"Because," said Jones, triumphant again, "the field-effect depends partly on temperature! The gases in the rocket-blast are hot, away up in the thousands of degrees. They don't have normal inertia, but they do have what you might call heat-inertia. They acquire a sort of fictitious mass when they get hot enough. So we carry along fuel that hasn't any inertia to speak of when it's cold, but acquires a lunatic sort of substitute for inertia when it's genuinely hot. So a ship can travel in a Dabney field!"

"I'm relieved," acknowledged Cochrane. "I thought you were about to tell me that we couldn't lift off the moon, and I was going to ask how we got here."

Jones smiled patiently.

"What I'm telling you now is that we can shoot rocket-blasts out of the Dabney field we make with the stern of the ship! Landing, we keep our fuel and the ship with next to no mass, and we shoot it out to where it does have mass, and the effect is practically the same as if we were pushing against something solid! And so we started off with fuel for maybe five or six landings and take-offs against Earth gravity. But with this new trick, we've got fuel for a couple of hundred!"

"Ah!" said Cochrane mildly. "This is the first thing you've said that meant anything to me. Congratulations! What comes next?"

"I thought you'd be pleased," said Jones. "What I'm really telling you is that now we've got fuel enough to reach the Milky Way."

"Let's not," suggested Cochrane, "and say we did! You've got a new star picked out to travel to?"

Jones shrugged his shoulders. In him, the gesture indicated practically hysterical frustration. But he said:

"Yes. Twenty-one light-years. Back on Earth they're anxious for us to check on sol-type suns and Earth-type planets."

"For once," said Cochrane, "I am one with the great scientific minds. Let's go over."

He made his way to the circular stairway leading down to the main saloon. On his clumsy way across the saloon floor to the communicator, he felt the peculiar sensation of the booster-current, which should have been a sound, but wasn't. It was the sensation which had preceded the preposterous leap of the space-ship away from Luna, when in a heart-beat of time all stars looked like streaks of light, and the ship traveled nearly two light-centuries.

Sunshine blinked, and then shone again in the ports around the saloon walls. The second shining came from a different direction—as if somebody had switched off one exterior light and turned on another—and at a different angle to the floor.

Cochrane reached the communicator. He felt no weight. He strapped himself into the chair. He switched on the vision-phone which sent radiation along the field to a balloon two hundred odd light-years from Earth—that was the balloon near the glacier planet—and then switched to the field traveling to a second balloon, then the last hundred seventy-odd light-years back to the moon, and then from Luna City down to Earth.

He put in his call. He got an emergency message that had been waiting for him. Seconds later he fought his way frantically through no-weight to the control-room again.

"Jamison! Bell!" he cried desperately. "We've got a broadcast due in twenty minutes! I lost track of time! We're sponsored on four continents and we damwell have to put on a show! What the devil! Why didn't somebody—"

Jamison said obviously from a blister-port where he swung a squat star-telescope from one object to another:

"Noo-o-o. That's a gas-giant. We'd be squashed if we landed there—though that big moon looks promising. I think we'd better try yonder."

"Okay," said Jones in a flat voice. "Center on the next one in, Al, and we'll toddle over."

Cochrane felt the ship swinging in emptiness. He knew because it seemed to turn while he felt that he stayed still.

"We've got a show to put on!" he raged. "We've got to fake something—."

Jamison looked aside from his telescope.

"Tell him, Bell," he said expansively.

"I wrote a script of sorts," said Bell apologetically. "The story-line's not so good—that's why I wanted a castaway narrative to put in it, though I wouldn't have had time, really. We spliced film and Jamison narrated it, and you can run it off. It's a kind of show. We ran it as a space-platform survey of the glacier-planet, basing it on pictures we took while we were in orbit around it. It's a sort of

123

travelogue. Jamison did himself proud. Alicia can find the tape-can for you."

He went back to his cameras. Cochrane saw a monstrous globe swing past a control-room port. It was a featureless mass of clouds, save for striations across what must be its equator. It looked like the Lunar Observatory pictures of Jupiter, back in the Sun's family of planets.

It went past the port, and a moon swam into view. It was a very large moon. It had at least one ice-cap—and therefore an atmosphere—and there were mottlings of its surface which could hardly be anything but continents and seas.

"We've got to put a show on!" raged Cochrane. "And now!"

"It's all set," Bell assured him. "You can transmit it. I hope you like it!"

Cochrane sputtered. But there was nothing to do but transmit whatever Bell and Jamison had gotten ready. He swam with nightmarelike difficulty back to the communicator. He shouted frantically for Babs. She and Alicia came. Alicia found the film-tape, and Cochrane threaded it into the transmitter, and bitterly ran the first few feet. Babs smiled at him, and Alicia looked at him oddly. Evidently, Babs had confided the consequence of their casting-away. But Cochrane faced an emergency. He began to check timings with far-distant Earth.

When the ship approached a second planet, Cochrane saw nothing of it. He was furiously monitoring the broadcast of a show in which he'd had no hand at all. From his own, professional standpoint it was terrible. Jamison spouted interminably, so Cochrane considered. Al, the pilot, was actually interviewed by an offscreen voice! But the pictures from space were excellent. While the ship floated in orbit, waiting to descend to pick up Babs and Cochrane, Bell had hooked his camera to an amplifying telescope and he did have magnificent shots of dramatic terrain on the planet now twenty light-years behind.

Cochrane watched the show in a mingling of jealousy and relief. It was not as good as he would have done. But fortunately, Bell and Jamison had stuck fairly close to straight travelogue-stuff, and close-up shots of vegetation and animals had been interspersed with the remoter pictures with moderate competence, if without undue imagination. An audience which had not seen many shows of the kind would be thrilled. It even amounted to a valid change

124

of pace. Anybody who watched this would at least want to see more and different pictures from the stars.

Halfway through, he heard the now-muffled noise of rockets. He knew the ship was descending through atmosphere by the steady sound, though he had not the faintest idea what was outside. He ground his teeth as—for timing—he received the commercial inserted in the film. The U. S. commercials served the purpose, of course. He could not watch the other pictures shown to residents of other than North America in the commercial portions of the show.

He was counting seconds to resume transmission when he felt the slight but distant impact which meant that the ship had touched ground. A very short time after, even the lessened, precautionary rocket-roar cut off.

Cochrane ground his teeth. The ship had landed on a planet he had not seen and in whose choice he had had no hand. He was humiliated. The other members of the ship's company looked out at scenes no other human eyes had ever beheld.

He regarded the final commercial, inserted into the broadcast for its American sponsor. It showed, purportedly, the true story of two girl friends, one blonde and one brunette, who were wall-flowers at all parties. They tried frantically to remedy the situation by the use of this toothpaste and that, and this deodorant and the other. In vain! But then they became the centers of all the festivities they attended, as soon as they began to wash their hair with Rayglo Shampoo.

Holden and Johnny Simms came clattering down from the control-room together. They looked excited. They plunged together toward the stair-well that would take them to the deck on which the airlock opened.

Holden panted,

"Jed! Creatures outside! They look like men!"

The communicator-screen faithfully monitored the end of the commercial. Two charming girls, radiant and lovely, raised their voices in grateful song, hymning the virtues of Rayglo Shampoo. There followed brisk reminders of the superlative, magical results obtained by those who used Rayglo Foundation Cream, Rayglo Kisspruf Lipstick, and Rayglo home permanent—in four strengths; for normal, hard-to-wave, easy-to-wave, and children's hair.

Cochrane heard the clanking of the airlock door.

CHAPTER NINE

HE MADE FOR THE CONTROL-ROOM, WHERE THE PORTS offered the highest and widest and best views of everything outside. When he arrived, Babs and Alicia stood together, staring out and down. Bell frantically worked a camera. Jamison gaped at the outer world. Al the pilot made frustrated gestures, not quite daring to leave his controls while there was even an outside chance the ship's landing-fins might find flaws in their support. Jones adjusted something on the new set of controls he had established for the extra Dabney field. Jones was not wholly normal in some ways. He was absorbed in technical matters even more fully than Cochrane in his own commercial enterprises.

Cochrane pushed to a port to see.

The ship had landed in a small glade. There were trees nearby. The trees had extremely long, lanceolate leaves, roughly the shape of grass-blades stretched out even longer. In the gentle breeze that blew outside, they waved extravagantly. There were hills in the distance, and nearby outcroppings of gray rocks. This sky was blue like the sky of Earth. It was, of course, inevitable that any colorless atmosphere with dust-particles suspended in it would establish a blue sky.

Holden was visible below, moving toward a patch of reed-like vegetation rising some seven or eight feet from the rolling soil. He had hopped quickly over the scorched area immediately outside the ship. It was much smaller than that made by the first landing on the other planet, but even so he had probably damaged his footwear to excess. But he now stood a hundred yards from the ship. He made gestures. He seemed to be talking, as if trying to persuade some living creature to show itself.

"We saw them peeping," said Babs breathlessly, coming beside Cochrane. "Once one of them ran from one patch

126

of reeds to another. It looked like a man. There are at least three of them in there—whatever they are!"

"They can't be men," said Cochrane grimly. "They can't!" Johnny Simms was not in sight. "Where's Simms?"

"He has a gun," said Babs. "He was going to get one, anyhow, so he could protect Doctor Holden."

Cochrane glanced straight down. The airlock door was open, and the end of a weapon peered out. Johnny Simms might be in a better position there to protect Holden by gun-fire, but he was assuredly safer, himself. There was no movement anywhere. Holden did not move closer to the reeds. He still seemed to be speaking soothingly to the unseen creatures.

"Why can't there be men here?" asked Babs. "I don't mean actually men, but—manlike creatures? Why couldn't there be rational creatures like us? I know you said so but—"

Cochrane shook his head. He believed implicitly that there could not be men on this planet. On the glacier planet every animal had been separately devised from the creatures of Earth. There were resemblances, explicable as the result of parallel evolution. By analogy, there could not be exactly identical mankind on another world because evolution there would be parallel but not the same. But if there were even a mental equal to men, no matter how unhuman such a creature might appear, if there were a really rational animal anywhere in the cosmos off of Earth, the result would be catastrophic.

"We humans," Cochrane told her, "live by our conceit. We demand more than animality of ourselves because we believe we are more than animals—and we believe we are the only creatures that are! If we came to believe we were not unique, but were simply a cleverer animal, we'd be finished. Every nation has always started to destroy itself every time such an idea spread."

"But we aren't only clever animals!" protested Babs. "We *are* unique!"

Cochrane glanced at her out of the corner of his eye. "Quite true."

Holden still stood patiently before the patch of reeds, still seemed to talk, still with his hands outstretched in what men consider the universal sign of peace.

There was a sudden movement at the back of the reed-patch, quite fifty yards from Holden. A thing which did look like a man fled madly for the nearest edge of wood-

127

land. It was the size of a man. It had the pinkish-tan color of naked human flesh. It ran with its head down, and it could not be seen too clearly, but it was startlingly manlike in outline. Up in the control-room Bell fairly yipped with excitement and swung his camera. Holden remained oblivious. He still tried to lure something out of concealment. A second creature raced for the woods.

Tiny gray threads appeared in the air between the airlock and the racing thing. Smoke. Johnny Simms was shooting zestfully at the unidentified animal. He was using that tracer ammunition which poor shots and worse sportsmen adopt to make up for bad marksmanship.

The threads of smoke seemed to form a net about the running things. They dodged and zig-zagged frantically. Both of them reached safety.

A third tried it. And now Johnny Simms turned on automatic fire. Bullets spurted from his weapon, trailing threads of smoke so that the trails looked like a stream from a hose. The stream swept through the space occupied by the fugitive. It leaped convulsively and crashed to earth. It kicked blindly.

Cochrane swore. Between the instant of the beginning of the creature's flight and this instant, less than two seconds had passed.

The threads which were smoke-trails drifted away. Then a new thread streaked out. Johnny Simms fired once more at his still-writhing victim. It kicked violently and was still.

Holden turned angrily. There seemed to be shoutings between him and Johnny Simms. Then Holden trudged around the reed-patch. There was no longer any sign of life in the still shape on the ground. But it was normal precaution not to walk into a jungle-like thicket in which unknown, large living things had recently been sighted. Johnny Simms fired again and again from his post in the airlock. The smoke which traced his bullets ranged to the woodland. He shot at imagined targets there. He fired at his previous victim simply because it was something to shoot at. He shot recklessly, foolishly.

Alicia, his wife, touched Jamison on the arm and spoke to him urgently. Jamison followed her reluctantly down the stairs. She would be going to the airlock. Johnny Simms, shooting at the landscape, might shoot Holden. A thread of bullet-smoke passed within feet of Holden's body. He turned and shouted back at the ship.

The inner airlock door clanked open. There was the

128

sound of a shot, and the dead thing was hit again. The bullet had been fired dangerously close to Holden. There were voices below. Johnny Simms bellowed enragedly.

Alicia cried out.

There was silence below, but Cochrane was already plunging toward the stairs. Babs followed closely.

When they rushed down onto the dining-room deck they found Alicia deathly white, but with a flaming red mark on her cheek. They found Johnny Simms roaring with rage, waving the weapon he'd been shooting. Jamison was uneasily in the act of trying to placate him.

"————!" bellowed Johnny Simms. "I came on this ship to hunt! I'm going to hunt! Try and stop me!"

He waved his weapon.

"I paid my money!" he shouted. "I won't take orders from anybody! Nobody can boss me!"

Cochrane said icily:

"I can! Stop being a fool! Put down that gun! You nearly shot Holden! You might still kill somebody! Put it down!"

He walked grimly toward Johnny Simms. Johnny was near the open airlock door. The outer door was open, too. He could not retreat. He edged sidewise. Cochrane changed the direction of his advance. There are people like Johnny Simms everywhere. As a rule they are not classed as unable to tell right from wrong unless they are rich enough to hire a psychiatrist. Yet a variable but always-present percentage of the human race ignores rules of conduct at all times. They are the handicap, the burden, the main hindrance to the maintainance or the progress of civilization. They are not consciously evil. They simply do not bother to act otherwise than as rational animals. The rest of humanity has to defend itself with police, with laws, and sometimes with revolts, though those like Johnny Simms have no motive beyond the indulgence of immediate inclinations. But for that indulgence Johnny would risk any injury to anybody else.

He edged further aside. Cochrane was white with disgusted fury. Johnny Simms went into panic. He raised his weapon, aiming at Cochrane.

"Keep back!" he cried ferociously. "I don't care if I kill you!"

And he did not. It was the stark senselessness which makes juvenile delinquents and Hitlers, and causes thugs and hoodlums and snide lawyers and tricky business men.

It was the pure perversity which makes sane men frustrate. It was an example of that infinite stupidity which is crime, but is also only stupidity.

Cochrane saw Babs pulling competently at one of the chairs at one of the tables nearby. He stopped, and Johnny Simms took courage. Cochrane said icily:

"Just what the hell do you think we're here for, anyhow?"

Johnny Simms' eyes were wide and blank, like the eyes of a small boy in a frenzy of destruction, when he has forgotten what he started out to do and has become obsessed with what damage he is doing.

"I'm not going to be pushed around!" cried Johnny Simms, more ferociously still. "From now on I'm going to tell you what to do—"

Babs swung the chair she had slid from its fastenings. It came down with a satisfying "*thunk*" on Johnny Simms' head. His gun went off. The bullet missed Cochrane by fractions of an inch. He plunged ahead.

Some indefinite time later, Babs was pulling desperately at him. He had Johnny Simms on the floor and was throttling him. Johnny Simms strangled and tore at his fingers,

Sanity came back to Cochrane with the effect of something snapping. He got up. He nodded to Babs and she picked up the gun Johnny Simms had used.

"I think," said Cochrane, breathing hard, "that you're a good sample of everything I dislike. The worst thing you do is make me act like you! If you touch a gun again on this ship, I'll probably kill you. If you get arrogant again, I will beat the living daylights out of you! Get up!"

Johnny Simms got up. He looked thoroughly scared. Then, amazingly, he beamed at Cochrane. He said amiably:

"I forgot. I'm that way. Alicia'll tell you. I don't blame you for getting mad. I'm sorry. But I'm that way!"

He brushed himself off, beaming at Alicia and Jamison and Babs and Cochrane. Cochrane ground his teeth. He went to the airlock and looked down outside.

Holden was bent over the creature Johnny Simms had killed. He straightened up and came back toward the ship. He went faster when the ground grew hot under his feet. He fairly leaped into the landing-sling and started it up.

"Not human," he reported to Cochrane when he slipped from the sling in the airlock. "There's no question about it when you are close. It's more nearly a bird than anything

130

else. It was warm-blooded. It has a beak. There are penguins on Earth that have been mistaken for men."

"I did a show once," said Cochrane coldly, "that had clips of old films of cockfighting in it. There was a kind of gamecock called Cornish Game that was fairly manshaped. If it had been big enough— Pull in the sling and close the lock. We're moving."

He turned away. Babs stood by Alicia, offering a handkerchief for Alicia to put to her cheek. Jamison listened unhappily as Johnny Simms explained brightly that he had always been that way. When he got excited he didn't realize what he was doing. He said almost with pride that he hadn't ever been any other way than that. He didn't really mean to kill anybody, but when he got excited—.

"What happened?" demanded Holden.

"Our little psychopath," said Cochrane in a grating voice, "put on an act. He threatened me with a rifle. He hit Alicia first. Jamison, trace that bullet-hole. See if it got through to the skin of the ship."

He started for the stairs again. Then he was startled by the frozen immobility of Holden. Holden's face was deadly. His hands were clenched. Johnny Simms said with a fine boyish frankness:

"I'm sorry, Cochrane! No hard feelings?"

"Yes," Cochrane snapped. "Hard feelings! I've got them!"

He took Holden's arm. He steered him up the steps. Holden resisted for the fraction of a second, and Cochrane gripped his arm tighter. He got him up to the deck above.

"If I'd been here," said Holden, unsteadily, "I'd have killed him—if he hit Alicia! Psychopath or no psychopath—"

"Shut up," said Cochrane firmly. "He shot at me! And in my small way I'm a psychopath too, Bill. My psychosis is that I don't like his kind of psychosis. I am psychotically devoted to sense and my possibly quaint idea of decency. I am abnormally concerned with the real world—and you'd better come back to it! Look here! I'm pathologically in revolt against such imbecilities as an overcrowded Earth and people being afraid of their jobs and people going crackpot from despair. You don't want me to get cured of that, do you? Then get hold of yourself!"

Bill Holden swallowed. He was still white. But he managed to grimace.

"You're right. Lucky I was outside. You're not a bad psychologist yourself, Jed."

"I'm better," said Cochrane cynically, "at putting on shows with scrap film-tape and dream-stuff. So I'm going to look at the films Bell took as we landed on this planet, and work out some ideas for broadcasts."

He went up another flight, and Holden went with him in a sort of still, unnatural calm. Cochrane ran the film-tape through the reversed camera for examination.

Outside, there waved long green tresses of extraordinarily elongated leaves. The patches of reed-like stuff stirred in the breeze. Jamison appeared in the control-room. He began to question Holden hopefully about the ground-cover outside. It was not grass. It was broad-leaved. There would be, Jamison decided happily, an infinitude of under-leaf forms of life. They would most likely be insects, and there would be carnivorous other insects to prey upon them. Some species would find it advantageous to be burrowing insects. There must be other kinds of birds than the giant specimens that looked like men at a distance, too. On the glacier planet there had been few birds but many furry creatures. Possibly the situation was reversed here, though of course it need not be . . .

"Hm," said Cochrane when the films were all run through. "Ice-caps and land and seas. Plenty of green vegetation, so presumably the air is normal for humans. Since you're alive, Holden, we can assume it isn't instantly fatal, can't we? The gravity's tolerable—a little on the light side, maybe, compared to the glacier planet."

He was silent, staring at the blank wall of the control-room. He frowned. Suddenly he said:

"Does anybody back on Earth know that Babs and I were castaways?"

"No," said Holden, still very quiet indeed. "Alicia ran the control-board. She told everybody you were too busy to be called to the communicator. It was queer with you away! Jamison and Bell tied themselves in chairs and spliced tape. Johnny, of course"—his voice was very carefully toneless—"wouldn't do anything useful. I was space-sick a lot of the time. But I did help Alicia figure out what to say on the communicator. There must be hundreds of calls backed up for you to take."

"Good!" said Cochrane. "I'll go take some of them. Jones, could we make a flit to somewhere else on this planet?"

Jones said negligently,

"I told you we've got fuel to reach the Milky Way. Where do you want to go?"

"Anywhere," said Cochrane. "The scenery isn't dramatic enough here for a new broadcast. We've got to have some lurid stuff for our next show. Things are shaping up except for the need of just the right scenery to send back to Earth."

"What kind of scenery do you want?"

"Animals preferred," said Cochrane. "Dinosaurs would do. Or buffalo or a reasonable facsimile. What I'd actually like more than anything else would really be a herd of buffalo."

Jamison gasped.

"Buffalo?"

"Meat," said Cochrane in an explanatory tone. "On the hoof. The public-relations job all this has turned into, demands a careful stimulation of all the basic urges. So I want people to think of steaks and chops and roasts. If I could get herds of animals from one horizon to another—."

"Meat-herds coming up," said Jones negligently. "I'll call you."

Cochrane did not believe him. He went down to the communicator again. He prepared to take the calls from Earth that had been backed up behind the emergency demand for an immediate broadcast-show that he'd met while the ship came to its landing. There was an enormous amount of business piled up. And it was slow work handling it. His voice took six seconds to pass through something over two hundred light-years of space in the Dabney field, and then two seconds in normal space from the relay in Lunar City. It was twelve seconds between the time he finished saying something before the first word of the reply reached him. It was very slow communication. He reflected annoyedly that he'd have to ask Jones to make a special Dabney field communication field as strong as was necessary to take care of the situation.

The rockets growled and roared outside. The ship lifted. Johnny Simms came storming up from below.

"My trophy!" he cried indignantly. "I want my trophy!"

Cochrane looked up impatiently from the screen.

"What trophy?"

"The thing I shot!" cried Johnny Simms fiercely. "I want to have it mounted! Nobody else ever killed anything like that! I want it!"

The ship surged upward more strongly. Cochrane said coldly:

"It's too late now. Get out. I'm busy."

He returned his eyes to the screen. Johnny Simms raced for the stairs. A little later Cochrane heard shoutings in the control-room. But he was too busy to inquire.

The ship drifted—with all the queasy sensation of no-weight—and lifted again, and then there was a fairly long period of weightlessness. At such times Holden would be greenish and sick and tormented by space-sickness. Which might be good for him at this particular time. For a long time, it seemed, there were alternating periods of lift and free fall, which in themselves were disturbing. Once the free fall lasted until Cochrane began to feel uneasy. But then the rockets roared once more and boomed loudly as if the ship were leaving the planet altogether.

But Cochrane was talking business. In part he bluffed. In part, quite automatically, he demanded much more than he expected to get, simply because it is the custom in busi-ness not to be frank about anything. Whatever he asked, the other man would offer less. So he asked too much, and the other man offered too little, each knowing in advance very nearly on what terms they would finally settle. Con-sidering the cost of beam-phone time to Lunar City, not to mention the extension to the stars, it was absurd, but it was the way business is done.

Presently Cochrane called Babs and Alicia and had them witness a tentative agreement, which had to be ratified by a board of directors of a corporation back on Earth. That board would jump at it, but the stipulation for possible can-cellation had to be made. It was mumbo-jumbo. Cochrane felt satisfyingly competent at handling it.

While the formalities were in progress, the ship surged and fell and swayed and surged again. Cochrane said rue-fully:

"I hate to ask you to work under conditions like this, Babs."

Babs grinned. He flushed a little.

"I know! When you were working for me I wasn't considerate."

"Who am I working for now?"

"Us," said Cochrane. Then he looked guiltily at Alicia. He felt embarrassment at having said anything in the least sentimental before her. Considering Johnny Simms, it was not too tactful. Her cheek, where it had been red, now

134

showed a distinct bruise. He said: "Sorry, Alicia—about Johnny."

"I got into it myself," said Alicia. "I loved him. He isn't really bad. If you want to know, I think he simply decided years ago that he wouldn't grow up pást the age of six. He was a rich man's spoiled little boy. It was fun. So he made a career of it. His family let him. I"—she smiled faintly, "I'm making a career of taking care of him."

"Something can be done even with a six-year-old," growled Cochrane. "Holden—. But he wouldn't be the best one to try."

"He definitely wouldn't be the best one to try," said Alicia very quietly.

Cochrane turned away. She knew how Bill Holden felt. Which might or might not be comforting to him.

The communicator again. The pictures of foot-high furry bipeds on the glacier planet had made a sensation on television. A toy-manufacturer wanted the right to make toys like them. The pictures were copyrighted. Cochrane matter-of-factly made the deal. There would be miniature extraterrestrial animals on sale in all toy-shops within days. Spaceways, Inc., would collect a royalty on each toy sold.

The rockets boomed, and lessened their noise, and wavered up and down again. Then there was that deliberate, crunching feel of the great landing-fins pressing into soil with all the ship's weight bearing down. The rockets ran on, drumming ever-so-faintly, for a little longer. Then they cut off.

"We've landed again! Let's see where we are!"

They went up to the control-room. Johnny Simms stood against the wall, sulking. He had managed his life very successfully by acting like a spoiled little boy. Now he had lost any idea of saner conduct. At the moment, he looked ridiculous. But Alicia had a bruised cheek and Cochrane could have been killed, and Holden had been in danger because Johnny Simms wanted to and insisted on acting like a rich man's spoiled little boy.

It occurred to Cochrane that Alicia would probably find recompense for her humiliation and pain in the little-boy penitence—exactly as temporary as any other little-boy emotion—when she and Johnny Simms were alone together.

The ship had come down close to the sunset-line of the planet. Away to the west there was the glint of blue sea.

135

Dusk was already descending here. There were smoothly contoured hills in view, and there was a dark patch of forest on one hilltop, and the trees at the woodland's edge had the same drooping, grass-blade-like foliage of the trees first seen. But there were larger and more solid giants among them. The ship had landed on a small plateau, and downhill from it a spring gushed out with such force that the water-surface was rounded by pressure from below. The water overflowed and went down toward the sea.

"I think we're all right," said Al, the pilot. But he stayed in his seat, in case the ship threatened to sway over. Cochrane inspected the outer world.

"Well?"

"We sighted what I think you want," said Jones. He looked dead-pan and yet secretly complacent. "Just watch."

The dusk grew deeper. Colorings appeared in the west. They were very similar to the sunset-colorings on Earth.

"Not many volcanoes here."

The amount of dust was limited, as on Earth. A great star winked into view in the east. It was as bright as Venus seen from Earth. It had a just-perceptible disk. Close to it, infinitely small, there was a speck of light which seemed somehow like a star. Cochrane squinted at it. He thought of the great gas-giant world he'd seen out a port on the way here. It had an attendant moon-world which itself had icecaps and seas and continents. He called Jamison.

"I think that's the planet," agreed Jamison. "We passed close by it. We saw it."

"It had a moon," observed Cochrane. "A big one. It looked like a world itself. What would it be like there?"

"Cooler than this," said Jamison promptly, "because it's farther from the sun. But it might pick up some heat from reflection from its primary's white clouds. It would be a fair world. It has oceans and continents and strings of foam-girt islands. But its sea is strange and dark and restless. Gigantic tides surge in its depths, drawn by the planetary collossus about which it swings. Its animal life——."

"Cut," said Cochrane dryly. "What do you really think? Could it be another inhabitable world for people to move to?"

Jamison looked annoyed at having been cut off.

"Probably," he said more prosaically. "The tides would be monstrous, though."

"Might be used for power," said Cochrane. "We'll see . . ."

Then Jones spoke with elaborate casualness:

"Here's something to look at. On the ground."

Cochrane moved to see. The dusk had deepened still more. The smooth, green-covered ground had become a dark olive. Where bare hillsides gave upon the sky, there were dark masses flowing slowly forward. The edges of the hills turned black, and the blackness moved down their nearer slopes. It was not an even front of darkness. There were patches which preceded the others. They did not stay distinct. They merged with the masses which followed them, and other patches separated in their places. All of the darkness moved without haste, with a sort of inexorable deliberation. It moved toward the ship and the valley and the gushing fountain and the stream which flowed from it.

"What on Earth—" began Cochrane.

"You're not on Earth," said Jones chidingly. "Al and I found 'em. You asked for buffalo or a reasonable facsimile. I won't guarantee anything; but we spotted what looked like herds of beasts moving over the green plains inland. We checked, and they seemed to be moving in this direction. Once we dropped down low and Bell got some pictures. When he enlarged them, we decided they'd do. So we lined up where they were all headed for, and here we are. And here they are!"

Cochrane stared with all his eyes. Behind him, he heard Bell fuming to himself as he tried to adjust a camera for close-up pictures in the little remaining light. Babs stood beside Cochrane, staring incredulously.

The darkness was beasts. They blackened the hillsides on three sides of the ship. They came deliberately, leisurely, onward. They were literally uncountable. They were as numerous as the buffalo that formerly thronged the western plains of America. In black, shaggy masses, they came toward the spring and its stream. Nearby, their heads could be distinguished. And all of this was perfectly natural.

The cosmos is one thing. Where life exists, its living creatures will fit themselves cunningly into each niche where life can be maintained. On vast green plains there will be animals to graze—and there will be animals to prey on them. So the grazing things will band together in herds for self-defense and reproduction. And where the ground is covered with broad-leaved plants, such plants will shelter innumerable tiny creatures, and some of them will be burrowers. So rain will drain quickly into those burrowings and not make streams. And therefore the drainage will reappear as springs, and the grazing animals will go to those springs to drink. Often, they will gather more densely at nightfall for greater protection from their enemies. They will even often gather at the springs or their over-flowing brooks. This will happen anywhere that plains and animals exist, on any planet to the edge of the galaxy, because there are laws for living things as well as stones.

Great dark masses of the beasts moved unhurriedly past the ship. They were roughly the size of cattle—which itself would be determined by the gravity of the planet, setting a maximum favorable size for grazing beasts with an ample food-supply. There were thousands and tens of thousands of them visible in the deepening night. They crowded to the gushing spring and to the stream that flowed from it. They drank. Sometimes groups of them waited patiently until the way to the water was clear.

"Well?" said Jones.

"I think you filled my order," admitted Cochrane.

The night became starlight only, and Cochrane impatiently demanded of Al or somebody that they measure the length of a complete day and night on this planet. The stars would move overhead at such-and-such a rate. So many degrees in so much time. He needed, said Cochrane —as if this order also could be filled—a day-length not more than six hours shorter or longer than an Earth-day.

Jones and Al conferred and prepared to take some sort of reading without any suitable instrument. Cochrane moved restlessly about. He did not notice Johnny Simms. Johnny had stood sullenly in his place, not moving to look out the window, ostentatiously ignoring everything and everybody. And nobody paid attention! It was not a matter to offend an adult, but it was very shocking indeed to a rich man's son who had been able to make a career of staying emotionally at a six-year-old level.

Cochrane's thoughts were almost feverish. If the day-length here was suitable, all his planning was successful. If it was too long or too short, he had grimly to look further—and Spaceways, Inc., would still not be as completely a success as he wanted. It would have been much simpler to have measured the apparent size of the local sun by any means available, and then simply to have timed the intervals between its touching of the horizon and its complete setting. But Cochrane hadn't thought of it at sunset.

Presently he wandered down to where Babs and Alicia

138

worked in the kitchen to prepare a meal. He tried to help. The atmosphere was much more like that in a small apartment back home than on a space-ship among the stars. This was not in any way such a journey of exploration as the writers of fiction had imagined. Jamison came down presently and offered to prepare some special dish in which he claimed to excel. There was no mention of Johnny Simms. Alicia, elaborately ignoring all that was past, told Jamison that Babs and Cochrane were now an acknowledged romance and actually had plans for marriage immediately the ship returned to Earth. Jamison made the usual inept jests suited to such an occasion.

Presently they called the others to dinner. Jones and Johnny Simms were long behind the others, and Jones' expression was conspicuously dead-pan. Johnny Simms looked sulkily rebellious. His sulking had not attracted attention in the control-room. He had meant to refuse sulkily to come to dinner. But Jones wouldn't trust him alone in the control-room. Now he sat down, scowling, and ostentatiously refused to eat, despite Alicia's coaxing. He snarled at her.

This, also, was not in the tradition of the behavior of voyagers of space. They dined in the over-large saloon of a ship that had never been meant really to leave the moon. The ship stood upright under strange stars upon a stranger world, and all about it outside there were the resting forms of thousands upon thousands of creatures like cattle. And the dinner-table conversation was partly family-style jests about Babs' and Cochrane's new romantic status, and partly about a television broadcast which had to be ready for a certain number of Earth-hours yet ahead. And nobody paid any attention to Johnny Simms, glowering at the table and refusing to eat.

It was a mistake, probably.

Much, much later, Cochrane and Babs were again in the control-room, and this time they were alone.

"Look!" said Cochrane vexedly. "Do you realize that I haven't kissed you since we got back on the ship? What happened?"

"You!" said Babs indignantly. "You've been thinking about something else every second of the time!"

Cochrane did not think about anything else for several minutes. He began to recall with new tolerance the insane antics of people he had been producing shows about. They had reason—those imaginary people—to act unreasonably.

But presently his mind was working again.

"We've got to make some plans for ourselves," he said. "We can live back on Earth, of course. We've already made a neat sum out of the broadcasts from this trip. But I don't think we'll want to live the way one has to live on Earth, with too many people there. I'd like——."

Somebody came clattering up the stairs from below.

"Johnny?" It was Bell. "Is he up here?"

Cochrane released Babs.

"No. He's not here. Why?"

"He's missing," said Bell apprehensively. "Alicia says he took a gun. A gun's gone, anyhow. He's vanished!"

Cochrane swore under his breath. A fool asserting his dignity with a gun could be a serious matter indeed. He switched on the control-room lights. He was not there. They went down and hunted over the main saloon. He was not there. Then Holden called harshly from the next deck down.

There was Alicia by the inner airlock door. Her face was deathly pale. She had opened the door. The outer door was open too—and it had not been opened since this last landing by anybody else. The landing-sling cables were run out. They swung slowly in the light that fell upon them from the inside of the ship.

A smell came in the opening. It was the smell of beasts. It was a musky, ammoniacal smell, somehow not alien even though it was unfamiliar. There were noises outside in the night. Grunting sounds. Snortings. There were such sounds as a vast concourse of grazing creatures would make in the night-time, when gathered by thousands and myriads for safety and for rest.

"He—went out," said Alicia desperately. "He meant to punish us. He's a spoiled little boy. We weren't nice to him. And—he was afraid of us too! So he ran away to make us sorry!"

Cochrane went to look out of the lock and to call Johnny Simms back. He gazed into absolute blackness on the ground. He felt a queasy giddiness because there was no hand-railing at the outer lock door and he knew the depth of the fall outside. He raged, within himself. Johnny Simms would feel triumphant when he was called. He would require to be pleaded with to return. He would pompously set terms for returning before he was killed . . .

Cochrane saw a flash of fire and the short streak of a tracer-bullet's patch before it hit something. He heard the

140

report of the gun. He heard a bellow of agony and then a scream of purest terror from Johnny Simms.

Then, from the ground, arose a truly monstrous tumult. Every one of the creatures below raised its voice in a horrible, bleating cry. The volume of sound was numbing—was agonizing in sheer impact. There were stirrings and clickings as of horns clashing against each other.

Another scream from Johnny Simms. He had moved. It appeared that he was running. Cochrane saw more gun-flashes, there were more shots. He clenched his hands and waited for the thunderous vibration that would be all this multitude of animals pounding through the night in blind stampede.

It did not come. There was only that bleating, horrible outcry as all the beasts bellowed in alarm and created this noise to frighten their assailants away.

Twice more there were shots in the night. Johnny Simms fired crazily and screamed in hysterical panic. Each time the shots and screaming were farther away.

There were no portable lights with which to make a search. It was unthinkable to go blundering among the beasts in darkness.

There was nothing to do. Cochrane could only watch and listen helplessly while the strong beast-smell rose to his nostrils, and the innumerable noises of unseen uneasy creatures sounded in his ears.

Inside the ship Alicia wept hopelessly. Babs tried in vain to comfort her.

CHAPTER TEN

THE SUN ROSE. COCHRANE NOTED THE TIME. IT WAS fourteen hours since sunset. The local day would be something more than an Earth-day in length. The manner of sunrise was familiar. There was a pale gray light in the sky. It strengthened. Then reddish colors appeared, and changed to gold, and the unnamed stars winked out one after another. Presently the nearer hillsides ceased to be black. There was light everywhere.

Alicia, white and haggard, waited to see what the light would show.

But there was heavy mist everywhere. The hill-crests were clear, and the edge of the visible woodland, and the top half of the ship's shining hull rose clear of curiously-tinted, slowly writhing fog. But everything else seemed submerged in a sea of milk.

But the mist grew thinner as the sun shone on it. Its top writhed to nothingness. All this was wholly commonplace. Even clouds in the sky were of types well-known enough. Which was, when one thought about it, inevitable. This was a Sol-type sun, of the same kind and color as the star which warmed the planet Earth. It had planets, like the sun of men's home world. There was a law—Bode's Law—which specified that planets must float in orbits bearing such-and-such relationships to each other. There must also be a law that planets in those orbits must bear such-and-such relationships of size to each other. There must be a law that winds must blow under ordinary conditions, and clouds form at appointed heights and times. It would be very remarkable if Earth were an exception to natural laws that other worlds obey.

So the strangeness of the morning to those who watched from the ship was more like the strangeness of an alien land on Earth than that of a wholly alien planet.

The lower dawnmist thinned. Gazing down, Cochrane

saw dark masses moving slowly past the ship's three metal landing-fins. They were the beasts of the night, moving deliberately from their bed-ground to the vast plains inland. There were bunches of hundreds, and bunches of scores. There were occasional knots of dozens only.

From overhead and through the mist Cochrane could not see individual animals too clearly, but they were heavy beasts and clumsy ones. They moved sluggishly. Their numbers dwindled. He saw groups of no more than four or five. He saw single animals trudging patiently away.

He saw no more at all.

Then the sunlight touched the inland hills. The last of the morning mist dissolved, and there were the dead bodies of two beasts near the base of the ship. Johnny Simms had killed them with his first panicky shots of the night. There was another dead beast a quarter-mile away.

Cochrane gave orders. Jones and Al could not leave the ship. They were needed to get it back to Earth, with full knowledge of how to make other star-ships. Cochrane tried to leave Babs behind, but she would not stay. Bell had loaded himself with a camera and film-tape besides a weapon, before Cochrane even began his organization. Holden was needed for an extra gun. Alicia, tearless and despairing, would not be left behind. Cochrane turned wryly to Jamison.

"I don't think Johnny was killed," he said. "He'd gotten a long way off before it happened, anyhow. We've got to hunt for him. With beasts like those of last night, there'll naturally be other creatures to prey on them. We might run into anything. If we don't get back, you get to the lawyers I've had representing Spaceways. They'll get rich off the job, but you'll end up rich, too."

"The best bet all around," said Jamison in a low tone, "would be to find him trampled to death."

"I agree," said Cochrane sourly. "But apparently the beasts don't stampede. Maybe they don't even charge, but just form rings to protect their females and young, like musk-oxen. I'm afraid he's alive, but I'm also afraid we'll never find him."

He marshalled his group. Jones had walkie-talkies ready, deftly removed for the purpose from space-suits nobody had used since leaving Lunar City—and Holden took one to keep in touch by. They went down in the sling, two at a time.

Cochrane regarded the two dead animals near the base

143

of the ship. They were roughly the size of cattle, and they were shaggy like buffalo. They had branching, pointed, deadly horns. They had hoofs, single hoofs, not cloven. They were not like any Earth animal. But horns and hoofs will appear in any system of parallel evolution. It would seem even more certain that proteins and amino acids and such compounds as hemoglobin and fat and muscle-tissue should be identical as a matter of chemical inevitability. These creatures had teeth and they were herbivorous. Bell photographed them painstakingly.

"Somehow," said Cochrane, "I think they'd be wholesome food. If we can, we'll empty a freezing-locker and take a carcass for tests."

Holden fingered his rifle unhappily. Alicia said nothing. Babs stayed close beside her. They went on.

They came to another dead animal a quarter-mile away. The ground was full of the scent and the hoofmarks of the departed herd. Bell photographed again. They did not stop. Johnny Simms had been this way, because of the carcass. He wasn't here now.

They topped the next rise in the ground. They saw two other slaughtered creatures. It was wholly evident, now, that these animals did not charge but only stood their ground when alarmed. Johnny Simms had fired blindly when he blundered into their groupings.

The last carcass they saw was barely two hundred yards from the one patch of woodland visible from the ship. Cochrane said with some grimness:

"If his eyes had gotten used to the darkness, he might have seen the forest and tried to get into it to get away from those animals."

And if Johnny Simms had not stopped short instantly he reached the woods and presumable safety, he would be utterly lost by now. There could be nothing less hopeful than the situation of a man lost on a strange planet, not knowing in what direction he had blundered on his first starting out. Even nearby, three directions out of four would be wrong. Farther away, the chance of stumbling on the way back to the ship would be nonexistent.

Alicia saw a human footprint on the trodden muck near the last carcass. It pointed toward the wood.

They reached the wood, and search looked hopeless. Then by purest chance they found a place where Johnny had stumbled and fallen headlong. He'd leaped up and fled crazily. For some fifteen yards they could track him by the trampled dried small growths he'd knocked down in his flight. Then there were no more such growths. All signs of his flight were lost. But they went on.

There were strangenesses everywhere, of which they could realize only a small part because they had been city-dwellers back on Earth. There was one place where trees grew like banyans, and it was utterly impossible to penetrate them. They swerved aside. There was another spot where giant trees like sequoias made a cathedral-like atmosphere, and it seemed an impiety to speak. But Holden reported tonelessly in the walkie-talkie, and assured Jones and Al and Jamison that all so far was well.

They heard a vast commotion of chattering voices, and they hoped that it might be a disturbance of Johnny Simms' causing. But when they reached the place there was dead silence. Only, there were hundreds of tiny nests everywhere. They could not catch a glimpse of a single one of the nests' inhabitants, but they felt that they were peeked at from under leaves and around branches.

Cochrane looked unhappy indeed. In cold blood, he knew that Johnny Simms had left the ship in exactly the sort of resentful bravado with which a spoiled little boy will run away from home to punish his parents. Quite possibly he had intended only to go out into the night and wait near the ship until he was missed. But he'd found himself among the unknown beasts. He'd gone into blind panic. Now he was lost indeed.

But one could not refuse to search for him simply because it was hopeless. Cochrane could not imagine doing any less than continuing to search as long as Alicia had hope. She might hope on indefinitely.

They heard the faint, distant, incisive sound of a shot. Holden's voice reported it in the walkie-talkie. Cochrane nodded brightly to Alicia and fired a shot in turn. He was relieved. It looked like everything would end in a commonplace fashion. The party from the ship headed toward the source of the other sound.

In half an hour Cochrane was about to fire again. But they heard the hysterical rat-tat-tat of firing. It seemed no nearer, but it could only be Johnny Simms.

Cochrane and Holden fired together for assurance to Johnny. Bell took pictures.

Again they marched toward where the shots had been fired. Again they trudged on for a long time. Seemingly, Johnny had moved away from them as they followed him.

They breasted a hill, and there was a breeze with the smell of water in it, and they saw that here the land sloped very gradually toward the sea, and the sea was in view. It was infinitely blue and it reached toward the most alluring of horizons. Between them and the sea there was only low-growing stuff, brownish and sparse. There was sand underfoot—a curious bluish sand. Only here and there did the dry-seeming vegetation grow higher than their heads.

More shots. Between them and the sea. Cochrane and Holden fired again.

"What the devil's the matter with the fool?" demanded Holden irritably. "He knows we're coming! Why doesn't he stand still or come to meet us?"

Cochrane shrugged. That thought was disturbing him too. They pressed forward, and suddenly Holden exclaimed. "That looks like a man! Two men!"

Cochrane caught the barest glimpse of something running about, far ahead. It looked like naked human flesh. It was the size of a man. It vanished. Another popped into view and darted madly out of sight. They did not see the newcomers.

"He shot something like that, back where we first landed," said Cochrane grimly. "We'd better hurry!"

They did hurry. There was a last flurry of shooting. It was automatic fire. It is not wise to shoot on automatic if one's ammunition is limited. Johnny Simms' firearm chattered furiously for part of a second. It stopped short. He couldn't have fired so short a burst. He was out of bullets.

They ran.

When they drew near him, a hooting set up. Things scattered away. Large things. Birds the size of men. They heard Johnny Simms screaming.

They came panting to the very beach, on which foam-tipped waves broke in absolutely normal grandeur. The sand was commonplace save for a slight bluish tint. Johnny Simms was out on the beach, in the open. He was down. He had flung his gun at something and was weaponless. He lay on the sand, shrieking. There were four ungainly, monstrous birds like oversized Cornish Game gamecocks pecking at him. Two ran crazily away at sight of the humans. Two others remained. Then they fled. One of them halted, darted back, and took a last peck at Johnny Simms before it fled again.

Holden fired, and missed. Cochrane ran toward the kicking, shrieking Johnny Simms. But Alicia got there first.

146

He was a completely pitiable object. His clothing had been almost completely stripped away in the brief time since his last burst of shots. There were wounds on his bare flesh. After all, the beak of a bird as tall as a man is not a weapon to be despised. Johnny Simms would have been pecked to death but for the party from the ship. He had been spotted and harried by a huntingpack of the ostrich-sized creatures at earliest dawn. A cooler-headed man would have stood still and killed some of them, then the rest would either have run away or devoured their slaughtered fellows. But Johnny Simms was not cool-headed. He had made a career of being a rich man's spoiled little boy. Now he'd had a fright great enough and an escape narrow enough to shatter the nerves of a normal man. To Johnny Simms, the effect was catastrophic.

He could not walk, and the distance was too great to carry him. Holden reported by walkie-talkie, and Jones proposed to butcher one of the animals Johnny had killed and put it in a freezer emptied for the purpose, and then lift the ship and land by the sea. It seemed a reasonable proposal. Johnny was surely not seriously wounded.

But that meant time to wait. Alicia sat by her husband, soothing him. Holden moved along the beach, examining the shells that had come ashore. He picked up one shell more glorious in its coloring than any of the pearl-making creatures of Earth. This shell grew neither in the flat spiral nor the cone-shaped form of Earth mollusks. It grew in a doubly-curved spiral, so that the result was an extraordinary, lustrous, complex sphere. Bell fairly danced with excitement as he photographed it with lavish pains to get all the colors just right.

Cochrane and Babs moved along the beach also. It was not possible to be apprehensive. Cochrane talked largely. Presently he was saying with infinite satisfaction:

"The chemical compounds here are bound to be the same! It's a new world, bigger than the glacier planet. Those beasts last night—if they're good food-stuff—will make this a place like the old west, and everybody envies the pioneers! This is a new Earth! Everything's so nearly the same—."

"I never," observed Babs, "heard of blue sand on Earth."

He frowned at her. He stooped and picked up a handful of the beach stuff. It was not blue. The tiny, sea-broken pebbles were ordinary quartz and granite rock. They would

147

have to be. Yet there was a blueness—The blue grains were very much smaller than the white and tan and gray ones. Cochrane looked closely. Then he blew. All the sand blew out of his hand except—at last—one tiny grain. It was white. It glittered greasily. Cochrane moved four paces and wetted his hand in the sea. He tried to wet the sand-grain. It would not wet.

He began to laugh.

"I did a show once," he told Babs, "about the old diamond-mines. Ever hear of them? They used to find diamonds in blue clay which was as hard as rock. Here, blue clay goes out from the land to under the waves. This is a tiny diamond, washed out by the sea! This is the last thing we need!" Then he looked at his watch. "We're due on the air in two hours and a half! Now we've got what we want! Let's go have Holden tell Jones to hurry!"

But Babs complained suddenly.

"Jed! What sort of life am I going to lead with you? Here we are, and—nobody can see us—and you don't even notice!"

Cochrane was penitent. In fact, they had to hurry back down the beach to join the others when the space-ship appeared as a silvery gleam, high in the air, and then came swooping down with fierce flames underneath it to settle a quarter-mile inland.

Bell had a picture of the tiny diamond by the time the ground was cool enough for them to re-enter the ship. The way he photographed it, against a background which had nothing by which its size could be estimated, the little white stone looked like a Kohinoor. It was two transparent pyramids set base to base, and he even got color-flashes from it. And Jamison, forewarned, took pictures from the air of the blue-sand areas. They showed the tint the one tiny diamond explained.

The broadcast was highly successful. It began with a four-minute commercial in which the evils of faulty elimination were discussed with infinite delicacy, and it was clearly proved—to an audience waiting to look beyond the stars—that only Greshham's Intestinal Emollient allowed the body to make full use of vitamins, proteins, and the very newest enzymatic foundation-substances which everybody needed for really perfect health. There followed the approach shots to this planet, shots of the great beast-herds on the plains, views of luxuriant, waving foliage, the tide of shaggy animals as they came at dusk to their drinking-

148

place, and there was an all-too-brief picturing of the blue-tinted soil which the last film-clip of all declared to be diamondiferous.

Cochrane's direction of this show was almost inspired. The views of the animal herd were calculated to make any member of his audience think in simultaneous terms of glamour and adventure—with perfect personal safety, of course!—and of steaks, chops and roasts. The more gifted viewers back on Earth might even envision filets mignon. The infinitesimal diamond with its prismatic glitterings, of course, roused cupidity of another sort.

There were four commercials cut into these alluring views, the last was superimposed upon a view Bell had taken of the sunset-colors. And it might have seemed that the television audience would confuse the charm of the new world as pictured with the product insistently praised. But the public was pretty well toughened up against commercials nowadays. It was not deceived. As usual, it only deceived itself.

But there was no deception about the fact that there was a new and unoccupied planet fit for human habitation. That was true. And the fretting overcrowded cities immediately became places where everybody made happy plans for his neighbor to move there. But the more irritable people would begin to think vaguely that it might be worth going to, for themselves.

The ship took off two hours after the broadcast. Part of that time was taken up with astrogational conferences with astronomers on Earth. Cochrane had this conference taped for the auxiliary broadcast-program in which the audience shared the problems as well as the triumphs of the star-voyagers. Cochrane wanted to get back to Earth. So far as television was concerned, it would be unwise. The ship and its crew would travel indefinitely without a lack of sponsors. But for once, Cochrane agreed entirely with Holden.

"We're heading back," he told Babs, "because if we keep on, people will accept our shows as just another superior kind of escape-entertainment. They'll have the dream quality of 'You Win a Million' and the lottery-shows. They'll be things to dream about but never to think of doing anything about. We're going to make the series disappointingly short, in order to make it more convincingly factual. We won't spin it out for its entertainment-value until it practically loses everything else."

"No," said Babs. She put her hand in his. She'd found it necessary to remind him, now and then.

So the ship started home. And it would not return direct to Earth—or Lunar City—for a very definite reason. Cochrane meant to have all his business affairs neatly wrapped up before landing. They could get another show or two across, and some highly involved contracts could be haggled to completion more smoothly if one of the parties —Spaceways, Inc.—was not available except when it felt like being available. The other parties would be more anxious.

So the astrogation-conference did not deal with a direct return to Earth, but with a small Sol-type star not too far out of the direct line. The Pole Star could have been visited, but it was a double star. Cochrane had no abstract scientific curiosity. His approach was strictly that of a man of business. He did the business.

There was, of course, a suitable pause not too far from the second planet—the planet of the shaggy beasts. They put out a plastic balloon with a Dabney field generator inside it. It would float in emptiness indefinitely. The field would hold for not less than twenty years. It would serve as a beacon, a highway, a railroad track through space for other ships planning to visit the third world now available to men. Ultimately, better arrangements could be made.

Jones was already ecstatically designing ground-level Dabney field installations. There would be Dabney fields extending from star to star. Along them, as along pneumatic tubes, ships would travel at unthinkable speeds toward absolutely certain destinations. True, at times they could not be used because of the bulk of planets between starting-points and landing-stations. But with due attention to scheduling, it would be a simple matter indeed to arrange for something close to commuters' service between star-clusters. He explained all this to Cochrane, with Holden listening in.

"Oh, surely!" said Cochrane cynically. "And you'll have tax-payers objecting because you make money. You'll be regulated out of existence. Were you thinking that Spaceways would run this transportation system you're planning, without cutting anybody else in on even the glory of it?"

Jones looked at him, dead-pan. But he was annoyed.

"I want some money," he said. "I thought we could get this thing set up, and then I could get myself a ship and facilities for doing some really original work. I'd like to

150

work something out and not have to sell the publicity-rights to it!"

"I'll arrange it," promised Cochrane. "I've got our law-yers setting up a deal right now. You're going to get as many tricky patents as you can on this field, and assign them all to Spaceways. And Spaceways is going to assign a sort of Chamber of Commerce for all the outer planets, and all the stuffed shirts in creation are going to leap madly to get honorary posts on it. And it will be practically beyond criticism, and it will have the public interest pas-sionately at its heart, and it will be practically beyond interference and it will be as inefficient as hell! And the more inefficient it is, the more it will have to take in to allow for its inefficiency—and for your patents it has to give us a flat cut of its gross! And meanwhile we'll get ours from the planets we've landed on and publicized. We've got customers. We've built up a market for our planets!"

"Eh?" said Jones in frank astonishment.

"We," said Cochrane, "rate as first inhabitants and therefore proprietors and governments of the first two planets ever landed on beyond Earth. When the Moon-colony was formed, there were elaborate laws made to take care of surviving nation prides and so on. Whoever first stays on a planet a full rotation is its proprietor and gov-ernment—until other inhabitants arrive. Then the govern-ment is all of them, but the proprietorship remains with the first. We own two planets. Nice planets. Glamorized planets, too! So I've already made deals for the hotel-concessions on the glacier world."

Holden had listened with increasing uneasiness. Now he said doggedly:

"That's not right, Jed! I don't mind making money, but there are things that are more important! Millions of people back home—hundreds of millions of poor devils—spend their lives scared to death of losing their jobs, not daring to hope for more than bare subsistence! I want to do something for them! People need hope, Jed, simply to be healthy! Maybe I'm a fool, but the human race needs hope more than I need money!"

Cochrane looked patient.

"What would you suggest?"

"I think," said Holden heavily, "that we ought to give what we've got to the world. Let the governments of the world take over and assist emigration. There's not one but will be glad to do it . . ."

"Unfortunately," said Cochrane, "you are perfectly right. They would! There have been resettlement projects and such stuff for generations. I'm very much afraid that just what you propose will be done to some degree somewhere or other on other planets as they're turned up. But on the glacier planet there will be hotels. The rich will want to go there to stay, to sight-see, to ride, to hunt, to ski, and to fly in helicopters over volcanoes. The hotels will need to be staffed. There will be guides and foresters and hunters. It will cost too much to bring food from Earth, so farms will be started. It will be cheaper to buy food from independent farmers than to raise it with hired help. So the farmers will be independent. There will have to be stores to supply them with what they need, and tourists with what they don't need but want. From the minute the glacier planet starts up as a tourist resort, there will be jobs for hundreds of people. It won't be long before there are jobs for thousands. There'll be a man-shortage there. Anybody who wants to can go there to work, and if he doesn't go there expecting a certified, psychologically conditioned environment, but just a good job with possible or probable advancement . . . That's the environment we humans want! Presently the hotels won't even be tourist hotels. They'll just be the normal hotels that exist everywhere that there are cities and people moving about among them! Then it won't be a tourist-planet, and tourists will be a nuisance. It'll be home for one hell of a lot of people! And they'll have made every bit of it themselves!"

Holden said uncomfortably:

"It'll be slow . . ."

"It'll be sure!" snapped Cochrane. "The first settlements in America were failures until the people started to work for themselves! Look at this planet we're leaving! How many people will come to work that silly diamond mine! How many will hunt to supply them with meat? How many will farm to supply the hunters and the miners with other food? And how many others will be along to run stores and manufacture things . . ." He made an impatient gesture. "You're thinking of encouraging people to move to the stars to make more room on Earth. You'd get nice passive colonists who'd obediently move because the long-hairs said it was wise and the government paid for it. I'm thinking of colonists who'll fight and quite possibly cheat

152

and lie a little to get jobs where they can take care of their families the way they want to! I want people to move to get what they want in spite of any discouragement anybody throws at them. Now shoo! I'm busy!"

Jones asked mildly:

"At what?"

"The latest proposed deal," said Cochrane impatiently, "is for rights to bore for oil. The uranium concessions are farmed out. Water-power is pending—not for cash, but a cut—and—."

Holden said uneasily:

"There's one other thing, Jed. All your plans and all your scheming could still be blocked if back on Earth they think we might bring plagues back to Earth. Remember Dabney suggested that? And some biologist or other agreed with him?"

Cochrane grinned.

"There's a diamond-mine. There are herds of what people will call cattle. There's food and riches. There's scenery and adventure. There's room to do things! Nobody could keep political office if he tried to keep his constituents from food and cash and adventure—even by proxy when they send expendable Cousin Albert out to see if he can make a living there. We've got to take reasonable precautions against germs, of course. We'll have trouble enforcing them. But we'll manage!"

Al called down from the control-room. The ship was sufficiently aligned, he thought, for their next stopping-place. He wanted Jones to charge the booster-circuit and flash it over. Jones went.

A little later there was the peculiar sensation of a sound that was not a sound, but was felt all through one. The result was not satisfactory. The ship was still in empty space, and the nearest star was still a star. There was a repetition of the booster-jump. Still not too good. Thereafter the ship drove, and jumped, and jumped, and drove.

Jamison came down to where Cochrane conducted business via communicator. He waited. Cochrane said:

"Dammit, I won't agree! I want twelve per cent or I take up another offer!—What?"

The last was to Jamison. Jamison said uneasily:

"We found another planet. About Earth-size. Ice-caps. Clouds. Oceans. Seas. Even rivers! But there's no green on it! It's all bare rocks!"

Cochrane thought concentratedly. Then he said impatiently:

"The whiskered people back home said that life couldn't have gotten started on all the planets suited for it. They said there must be planets where life hasn't reached, though they're perfectly suited for it. Make a landing and try the air with algae like we did on the first planet."

He turned back to the communicator.

"You reason," he snapped to a man on far-away Earth, "that all this is only on paper. But that's the only reason you're getting a chance at it! I'll guarantee that Jones will install drives on ships that meet our requirements of space-worthiness—or government standards, whichever are strictest—for ten per cent of your company stock plus twelve per cent cash of the cost of each ship. Nothing less!"

He heard the rockets make the louder sound that was the symptom of descent against gravity.

The world was lifeless. The ship had landed on bare stone, when Cochrane looked out the control-room ports. There had been trouble finding a flat space on which the three landing-fins would find a suitable foundation. It had taken half an hour of maneuvering to locate such a place and to settle solidly on it. Then the look of things was appalling.

The landing-spot was a naked mass of what seemed to be basalt polygons, similar to the Giants' Causeway of Ireland back on Earth. There was no softness anywhere. The stone which on other planets underlay soil, here showed harshly. There was no soil. There was no microscopic life to nibble at rocks and make soil in which less minute life could live. The nudity of the stones led to glaring colors everywhere. The colors were brilliant as nowhere else but on Earth's moon. There was no vegetation at all.

That was somehow shocking. The ship's company stared and stared, but there could be no comment. There was a vast, dark sea to the left of the landing-place. Inland there were mountains and valleys. But the mountains were not sloped. There were heaps of detritus at the bases of their cliffs, but it was simply detritus. No tiniest patch of lichen grew anywhere. No blade of grass. No moss. No leaf. Nothing.

The air was empty. Nothing flew. There were clouds, to be sure. The sky was even blue, though a darker blue than Earth's, because there was no vegetation to break stone down to dust, or to form dust by its own decay.

154

The sea was violently active. Great waves flung themselves toward the harsh coastline and beat upon it with insensate violence. They shattered into masses of foam. But the foam broke—too quickly—and left the surging water dark again. Far down the line of foam there were dark clouds, and rain fell in masses, and lightning flashed. But it was a scene of desolation which was somehow more horrible even than the scarred and battered moon of Earth.

Cochrane looked out very carefully. Alicia came to him, a trifle hesitant.

"Johnny's asleep now. He didn't sleep at first, and while we were out of gravity he was unhappy. But he went off to sleep the instant we landed. He needs rest. Could we—just stay landed here until he catches up on sleep?"

Cochrane nodded. Alicia smiled at him and went away. There was still the mark of a bruise on her cheek. She went down to where her husband needed her. Holden said dourly:

"This world's useless. So is her husband."

"Wait till we check the air," said Cochrane absently.

"I've checked it," Holden told him indifferently. "I went in the port and sniffed at the cracked outer door. I didn't die, so I opened the door. There is a smell of stone. That's all. The air's perfectly breathable. The ocean's probably absorbed all soluble gases, and poisonous gases are soluble. If they weren't, they couldn't be poisonous."

"Mmmmmm," said Cochrane thoughtfully.

Jamison came over to him.

"We're not going to stay here, are we?" he asked. "I don't like to look at it. The moon's bad enough, but at least nothing could live there! Anything could live here. But it doesn't! I don't like it!"

"We'll stay here at least while Johnny has a nap. I do want Bell to take all the pictures he can, though. Probably not for broadcast, but for business reasons. I'll need pictures to back up a deal."

Jamison went away. Holden said without interest:

"You'll make no deals with this planet! This is one you can do what you like with! I don't want any part of it!"

Cochrane shrugged.

"Speaking of things you don't want any part of—what about Johnny Simms? Speaking as a psychiatrist, what effect will that business of being in the dark all night and nearly being pecked to death—what will it do to him?

155

Are psychopaths the way they are because they can't face reality, or because they've never had to?"

Holden stared away down the incredible, lifeless coastline at the distant storm. There was darkness under many layers of cloud. The sea foamed and lashed and instantly was free of foam again. Because there were no plankton, no animalcules, no tiny, gluey, organic beings in it to give the water the property of making foam which endured. There was thunder, yonder in the storm, and no ear heard it. Over a vast world there was sunshine which no eyes saw. There was night in which nothing rested, and somewhere dawn was breaking now, and nothing sang.

"Look at that, Jed," said Holden heavily. "There's a reality none of us wants to face! We're all more or less fugitives from what we are afraid is reality. That is real, and it makes me feel small and futile. So I don't like to look at it. Johnny Simms didn't want to face what one does grow up to face. It made him feel futile. So he picked a pleasanter role than realist."

Cochrane nodded.

"But his unrealism of last night put him into a very realistic mess that he couldn't dodge! Will it change him?"

"Probably," said Holden without any expression at all in his voice. "They used to put lunatics in snake-pits. When they were people who'd taken to lunacy for escape from reality, it made them go back to reality to escape from the snakes. Shock-treatments used to be used, later, for the same effect. We're too soft to use either treatment now. But Johnny gave himself the works. The odds are that from now on he will never want to be alone even for an instant, and he will never again quite dare to be angry with anybody or make anybody angry. You choked him and he ran away, and it was bad! So from now on I'd guess that Johnny will be a very well-behaved little boy in a grown man's body." He said very wryly indeed, "Alicia will be very happy, taking care of him."

A moment later he added:

"I look at that set-up the way I look at the landscape yonder."

Cochrane said nothing. Holden liked Alicia. Too much. It would not make any difference at all. After a moment, though, he changed the subject.

"I think this is a pretty good bet, this planet. You think it's no good. I'm going to talk to the chlorella companies. They grow edible yeast in tanks, and chlorella in vats, and

156

they produce an important amount of food. But they have to grow the stuff indoors and they have a ghastly job keeping everything sterile. Here's a place where they can sow chlorella in the oceans! They can grow yeast in lakes, out-of-doors! Suppose they use this world to grow monstrous quantities of unattractive but useful foodstuff—in a way—wild? It will be good return-cargo material for ships taking colonists out to our other planets.—I suppose," he added meditatively, "they'll ship it back in bulk, dried."

Holden blinked. He was jolted out of even his depression.

"Jed!" he said warmly. "Tell that to the world—prove that—and—people will stop being afraid! They won't be afraid of starving before they can get to the stars! Jed—Jed! This is the thing the world needs most of all!"

But Cochrane grimaced.

"Maybe," he admitted it. "But I've tasted the stuff. I think it's foul! Still, if people want it . . ."

He went back down to the communicator to contact the chlorella companies of Earth, to find out if there was any special data they would need to pass on the proposal.

* * * * *

And so presently the ship took off for home. It landed on the moon first, and Johnny Simms was loaded into a space-suit and transferred to Lunar City, where he could live without being extradited back to Earth. He wouldn't stay there. Alicia guaranteed that. They'd move to the glacier planet as soon as hotels were built. Maybe some day they'd travel to the planet of the shaggy beasts. Johnny would never be troublesome again. He was pathetically anxious, now, to have people like him, and stay with him, and not under any circumstances be angry with him or shut him away from them. Alicia would now have a full-time occupation keeping people from taking advantage of him.

But the ship went back to Earth. And on Earth Jamison became the leading television personality of all time, describing and extrapolating the delicious dangers and the splendid industrial opportunities of star-travel. Bell was his companion and co-star. Presently Jamison conceded privately to Cochrane that he and Bell would need shortly to take off on another journey of exploration with some other expedition. Neither of them thought to retire, though they were well-off enough. They were stock-holders in the Spaceways company, which guaranteed them a living.

Cochrane put Spaceways, Inc., into full operation. He fought savagely against personal publicity, but he worked himself half to death. He spent hours every day in frenzied haggling, and in the cynical examination of deftly booby-trapped business proposals. His lawyers insisted that he needed an office—he did—and presently he had four secretaries and there developed an entire hierarchy of persons under him. One day his chief secretary told him commiseratingly that somebody had waited two hours past appointment-time to see him.

It was Hopkins, who had not been willing to interrupt his dinner to listen to a protest from Cochrane. Hopkins was still exactly as important as ever. It was only that Cochrane was more so.

It woke Cochrane up. He stormed, to Babs, and ruthlessly cancelled appointments and abandoned or transferred enterprises, and made preparations for a more satisfactory way of life.

They went, in time, to the Spaceways terminal, to take ship for the stars. The terminal was improvised, but it was busy. Already eighteen ships a day went away from there in Dabney fields. Eighteen others arrived. Jones was already off somewhere in a ship built according to his own notions. Officially he was doing research for Spaceways, Inc., but actually nobody told him what to do. He puttered happily with improbable contrivances and sometimes got even more improbable results. Holden was already off of Earth. He was on the planet of the shaggy beasts, acting as consultant on the cases of persons who arrived there and became emotionally disturbed because they could do as they pleased, instead of being forced by economic necessity to do otherwise.

But this day Babs and Cochrane went together into the grand concourse of the Spaceways terminal. There were people everywhere. The hiring-booths of enterprises on the three planets now under development took applications for jobs on those remote worlds, and explained how long one had to contract to work in order to have one's fare paid. Chambers of Commerce representatives were prepared to give technical information to prospective entrepreneurs. There were reservation-desks, and freight-routing desks, and tourist-agency desks . . .

"Hmmm," said Cochrane suddenly. "D'you know, I

158

haven't heard of Dabney in months! What happened to him?"

"Dabney?" said Babs. She beamed. Women in the terminal saw the clothes she was wearing. They did not recognize her—Cochrane had kept her off the air—but they envied her. She felt very nice indeed. "Dabney?—Oh, I had to use my own judgment there, Jed. You were so busy! After all, he was scientific consultant to Spaceways. He did pay Jones cold cash for fame-rights. When everything else got so much more important than just the scientific theory, he got in a terrible state. His family consulted Doctor Holden, and we arranged it. He's right down this way!"

She pointed. And there was a splendid plate-glass office built out from the wall of the grand concourse. It was elevated, so that it was charmingly conspicuous. There was a chastely designed but highly visible sign under the stairway leading to it. The sign said; *"H. G. Dabney, Scientific Consultant."*

Dabney sat at an imposing desk in plain view of all the thousands who had shipped out and the millions who would ship out in time to come. He thought, visibly. Presently he stood up and paced meditatively up and down the office which was as eye-catching as a gold-fish bowl of equal size in the same place. He seemed to see someone down in the concourse. He could have recognized Cochrane, of course. But he did not.

He bowed. He was a great man. Undoubtedly he returned to his wife each evening happily convinced that he had done the world a great favor by permitting it to glimpse him.

Cochrane and Babs went on. Their baggage was taken care of. The departure of a ship for the stars, these days, was much less complicated and vastly more comfortable than it used to be when a mere moon-rocket took off.

When they were in the ship, Babs heaved a sigh of absolute relief.

"Now," she said zestfully, "now you're retired, Jed! You don't have to worry about anything! And so now I'm going to try to make you worry about me—not worry about me, but think about me!"

"Of course," said Cochrane. He regarded her with honest affection. "We'll take a good long vacation. First on the glacier planet. Then we'll build a house somewhere in the hills back of Diamondville . . ."

"Jed!" said Babs accusingly.

"There's a fair population there already," said Cochrane, apologetically. "It won't be long before a local television station will be logical. I was just thinking, Babs, that after we get bored with loafing, I could start a program there. Really sound stuff. Not commercial. And of course with the Dabney field it could be piped back to Earth if any sponsor wanted it. I think they would . . ."

Presently the ship with Babs and Cochrane among its passengers took off to the stars. It was a perfectly routine flight. After all, star-travel was almost six months old. It wasn't a novelty any longer.

Operation Outer Space was old stuff.

THE END.